PUBLIC PROPERTY

Public Property

And Other Stories

Heather Colley

Paperback ISBN: 9781947175884

Cover design by Jacob Arms

Published by Serving House Books
Lawrence Landing Company
Raleigh, North Carolina 27609
United States of America
www.servinghousebooks.com

Serving House Books is a proud member of

Independent Book Publishers Association
 and
Community of Literary Magazines and Presses

CONTENTS

For mom, with all my love

PUBLIC PROPERTY

"And where was the blood found, exactly?"
"Well that's the thing, right. Everywhere, in a way."
"Everywhere?"
"In a type of way. But it was *deliberate*."
"Deliberately everywhere?"
"So."
"And we're sure about those responsible?"
"Yeah. It's always the teenage fucking girls."

***

In her classroom Jane cried.

I stood and said things that you're meant to say when a friend is crying. I said things like, it will really all be alright, in the end. "When is the end?" she said. I don't know, I said. Not for a long time. "Yeah," she said. "That's the problem."

It didn't help her mood that we were public property. We are mothers and fathers and aunties and social workers and big brothers and sisters, and coaches and mentors, and therapists and doctors, and psychiatrists, and real estate agents and customs officials and lawyers, and representatives and lobbyists, and key constituents of the political debate, and thinkers and scholars and leaders, and custodians and janitors and mental health professionals, and the problem for me, it has always seemed – is that I am just a woman. It is no longer enough, unfortunately. I must be woman and everybody, or else I am not woman at all. We are entirely public. This is why

Beau and Ashleigh stormed Jane's room that morning and stormed on till they reached her desk, where she was trying to wipe her tears with the wetness of more tears. Tears have tears. But because Beau and Ashleigh were 16 years old, they didn't notice. Many teenagers reject curiosity. If you're not disengaged, you're not modern. And because we are teachers, we tolerate it. Nobody wanting us for anything much; our arms are extensions of the filing cabinet and our toes figments of the cleaning cupboard.

We are inanimate objects for a lot of the time.

"Something has happened," Ashleigh said.

As things do, I said. They looked at me like I was out of line.

"What's wrong, girls?"

Jane was a natural-born teacher. She claimed that she could not see herself doing anything else. And while this was intended to imply a sort of inherently philanthropic nature, I suspected that it was more to do with complacency. It is so easy to do the easy thing, especially when you do it every day. That is why teachers stay teachers stay teachers. I sometimes feel that the sidewalk never ends to the grave. Then I'll be looking at it and I'll think oh *fuck,* my whole life has been a pursuit of the professional. I've despised it.

And now the girls told a manic story that involved bathrooms and blood and puberty.

Another working day begun, and already so tired tired tired.

***

I had to go to the pharmacy during my lunch.

The Academy was toward the top of High Street, which was a hill. Life happened on either side of it. Here was the roadman just inside the coffee shop. Here was the barista, training another barista. Here was the trainee barista, reading an employee handbook. Somewhere was the writer who wrote it. Somewhere near them was the Executive who demanded it, and somewhere near them was the salesman who supported it. Elsewhere was a man getting rich.

I was nowhere to be found. That was how it was, then: Life was a lovely bustle all around, and I with not a single toe through its door.

The pharmacy was sterile and unlovely. A line of people stood extended outward from the sign: PRESCRIPTION PICKUP. Everything ticks in a pharmacy. Toes, pens. The heart at certain rhythms.

There had recently been a complication. It began when I started this medication, and it happened again on that morning, as I stood before the pharmacist. They can't just give a refill and send me off back down the road. I suspect that this is their conspiratorial punishment. Your brain, they're saying. It's not quite right. It's a bit *off,* your brain. It's gotten so tired; it's gotten so weepy! Sorry – what was your last name again?

"Bird."

"B – e—a – r –d?"

"Bird."

"Sorry?"

"Like a canary?"

"I thought it was bird."

"Then why did you have to ask?"

"So."

"B-i-r-d."

"Date of birth?"

Another pharmacist joined. He asked: "Date of birth?" as his colleague wandered away.

"October the 27th 1995."

"I'm sorry. What was the last name?"

"Bird."

"That's pretty."

"And then the date of birth is October the 27th. 1995."

"First name?"

"Mary."

"Spell it."

"M—a—r—y."

"So, it's one month supply? Of this –"

***

I made it back in time for the lesson, the start of which was unusually uneventful. I settled into a suspicious calm.

I assigned a creative writing task. I instructed the students to compose a short story about a scene which involved *exuberance,* a word which appeared on that month's spelling list.

The story can be real or made up, I said. Or a mix of both. You must use literary devices. Metaphors, similes, allegories, and so on. You must work silently. You have twenty-seven minutes from now. No hands for the first ten minutes. I wrote these instructions on the board.

Begin, I said. Seven hands went up. I nodded to the first one, which belonged to Dexter.

"Miss, are we allowed to make it up?"

"Yes."

Two hands went down as another shot up. I nodded toward the new one, which belonged to Millie.

"But does it have to be made up?"

"No. It can be real. It is up to you."

I nodded toward Kieran, who suffered from deep anxiety and had a "leaving pass" as a consequence. He could exit the room without permission if emotionally overwhelmed.

"Miss, how much time do we have?"

"About twenty-one minutes now."

"Oh. Really?"

I nodded. His hand shot back up, then down. I said, "No questions for the next ten minutes. If you want *individual guidance,* reread your work, then I will help."

Kieran put his hand down. He looked straight at me, our glares meeting in the stinky space of the room's cluttered prepubescence. He pulled his card from the inside of the blazer, I nodded, and he exited the room. I prepared myself.

"Miss, why is he allowed to up and leave?" This from Dexter.

"He's got a pass. Working silently."

"I've got a pass."

"No. We're working silently now.".

There was a knock at the door. Nadine was the new internal social worker, and she appeared in my doorframe at least twice per day.

"Sorry about this, Miss."

She looked outward across the audience.

"I need to borrow Joanne. Would that be alright, Miss?"

Joanne's bag was packed and her foot out the door

before Nadine had finished delivering her question. Unspoken, it was always alright. Yes, thank you, Mrs. Turner, I said. I turned back inward.

"Miss?"

"Working silently now, Dexter."

"I don't have any ideas."

"Anything that interests you."

"Nothing interests me, Miss."

I went toward his desk. Dexter was capable once he set off; the trouble was that he rarely ever started, which convinced him that there was no way through or around or over. He liked to stay behind, where nobody expected anything much.

"Anything interesting happen this weekend that you would like to write about?"

"Nothing that you would like to read about."

I faced Dexter with my back to the door. A compromised position. The school was made of glass: the classroom doors, the walls of everything. The only opaque spaces which still retained the pre-remodel concrete were the offices of those in senior leadership.

This is why standing with your back to the classroom entrance is a risk. The leadership spend a significant amount of time pacing the halls and staring freely through the glass of classrooms, serializing teachers' mistakes and shortcomings and students' failures, depressions, episodes.

I abandoned Dexter still without ideas or desire. Paced once around the room, pretended to read over bits of stories. Kieran had returned by the time I arrived at his desk, front right. He was our star. He scored well on his exams but his creative writing was stifled.

"Can I see what you've got?"

He handed me his workbook, half a page filled, the writing getting bigger and more robust the farther down it went.

It was the middle of the night. It is hard to feel <u>exuberant</u> in the middle of the night. So, I didn't. Then I got up. Something was at my window. What was it? Tap. Tap. Tap. Oh my god, I think.

I scanned the rest, landing with satisfaction at his conclusion – *Was it all a dream?*

"It was," he tells me.

I stared at it. He stared at me staring at it.

"Miss."

"Miss."

"Miss."

Pens clicked, bags opened, flirtations began again. I looked toward the glass.

He was approaching. His attempts to appear meandering were pathetic. Dr Halls opened the door, shot his head in, stared directly at Dexter, who stared directly back.

I looked again at Kieran's story.

"Lovely," I said. "That's brilliant." The silence held and quivered. "I like your use of metaphors. The ending is evocative."

Kieran smiled as Dr Halls shut the door. They ruptured, then. Papers ripped; pens bled. I let the chaos onward. It is sometimes nice to let it force its way in, to let it climb inward and around. I dismissed them early, slumped down for a moment, then walked over to Jane's room, where she also had a free period, and where she'd again begun to cry.

***

"They're sometimes manic, and sometimes not."

"That's year 10," said Jane.

"Sure. Highly hormonal."

"Especially this lot."

"Yeah?"

"Yeah. There's been a development in the Year 10 girls' bathroom story."

"Yeah?"

"Yeah. Menstrual."

"You're joking."

"Nope. They sent it off somewhere. I heard from Laura who heard from Josh. Who was told by Dr Halls."

"So it was actual writing?"

"Yep. Various things, in blood."

"Want a coffee?"

"Yeah."

We wandered down the English hall into Math and Science. Then into the staff room, where we made coffees from stale dust. We wandered back toward the Humanities side, penetrating through the glass of the Math rooms as we went. Dr Halls passed us by before we reached English. His eyes went in and all around.

***

My year 7s were characteristically early, lined up outside. I went in and locked the door. I placed a copy of *Peter Pan* on each desk. An odd choice, I thought. Jane disagreed. "It's easy enough for them to follow," she'd say. "It's a part of their popular culture, sort of. It's pretty."

"Is it?" I'd say. "Sometimes I think it's revolting."

"Yeah," she'd respond. "I guess that's the beauty of interpretation."

After my Year 7s I had three back-to-back Year 8 grammar lessons, each of which were the exact same as the one before.

I started to feel the cloud. It always came back around toward the end of the school day. It made children despicable. It made me despicable. Something welled up in my womb. The posters on the walls were farcical propaganda. Macbeth and Scrooge and Miss Havisham cackled in gross laughter. I told my final year 8 group that we'd finish with a film, and pulled up the original *Wizard of Oz*. Everyone sunk into it. I closed my eyes till final bell.

***

Jane often worked until after 5pm, and so we never left school together. I always left as early as possible, once the children vacated. I despised speaking to them after hours, when I was not myself anymore. Just before 5pm I glided into the bathroom to change into gym clothes. I felt the hormonal warmth. My fingers are small. They were covered in brightness. It was beautiful. With my pointer finger, I began to write.

"CHANGE IS A GOOD THING!"

"I'll tell you where the mess was found."

Caroline beside me, a shift in her wooden auditorium seat that signified her suppressed laughter.

"On the floor of the principal's office," he said. He always seemed to exist in the third person, at a deep distance from himself. I danced a fingertip around the naked crown of my head, where scabs had emerged on my scalp. Picked one, flicked it.

"It wreaks of dill," continued Dr. Amis. "Multi-day-old dill."

I thought about my lesson plan for *Jane Eyre* as the principal went on about the soup vandalism. This was the second similar offense. After the morning meeting, I unlocked my classroom door, flicked on the lights so that the black turned to grey.

Caroline emerged in the doorframe, said, "Did you hear yet about next term's cultural initiative?"

"I haven't checked my email."

"Same. Where are you in *Jane Eyre?*"

"Around the middle. They find it boring. Yours?"

"Yeah. Dull as shit. What do you think of the soup?"

"It's the kids," I said.

"But who?"

"If I had to guess, the girls who vape in the bathroom, the juniors."

"Yeah." She opened her laptop, showed me the title of her lesson plan. *Jane Eyre: Forward Directions.*

"What does that even mean?" I asked.

"I don't know. And yeah." She clickclacked on the keys.

"You're right about the soup. It's always the teenage girls."

Like most days at school, there wasn't much to say about that one. The kids didn't want to read, and I didn't want to read to them. Metaphor, I said. Simile. Imagery. *Simile*, they spat back, as if it were so vile and rotten.

I stopped at the pharmacy on the walk home. The prescription line stretched around the shop. I slinked to the end of the queue, next to the cartons of grapes. They gave off a pre-rot smell, as if they all needed stuffing down the nearest gullet. The depths of the cartons were a packed web of grapeish guts and nascent fuzz. I felt uncomfortable beside them, as if the mould could creep into me. I wished for the queue to move, and it didn't. Picked up a newspaper; got depressed and put it down.

My turn.

"For Bertha," I said. "Twentieth June."

He pivoted round to the shelf of pills.

"Last name?"

I told him.

He stood before the wall of prescription medication, started to look around and in corners. I got itchy.

"Uh," I said. "B – E – R – T – H – A?"

He shuffled some scripts around again, and then he had one in his hand, but didn't place it on the counter.

"Uh. Are you sure you're spelling it right?"

"My name?"

An embarrassed understanding overtook me.

"Oh, no. I'm sorry. It should be under, uh, Badra. B – A – D – R – A. Long day. Ha-ha. Sorry."

He nodded. I sensed weight shifting behind me. An idiotic mistake. The fuzzy, ruptured grapes crept under the dried blood on my scalp, and I picked at them the whole walk home.

Once inside the apartment, I slipped off my jacket and put on my headscarf. For all the long day of nudity I want to feel covered at least sometimes. At school I am utterly naked. Beyond naked – without clothes, and without skin. Always I am stared through, looked at, peered into. So in the mirrors of my home, I wish to be covered – and is that such a deep dark thing? If I cannot be covered in the school building, shan't I cover in my bedroom?

In bed I thought of how my mom would react to this behaviour. Shame, she'd say. Be proud of who you are. Or some other such aphorism. The language of aphorisms and proverbs is broken, I'd think. It's shattered. It no longer works, no longer fits. Can't you see?

I did this, sometimes. Imaginary chats with my mother. They usually ended with berating, me to myself. To coax myself to sleep I pawed at my skin, at the bedcovers, like a cat does on cloth when it's been ripped from the belly too early. I felt raised patches on my thighs and on my upper arms, waxy and irregular like chopped up celery. Another bout of eczema, or a rash. Set my alarm for school.

Woke up and my fingertips went straight to the welts on my skin, still there. Another school day; more nakedness. Pulled on my outfit. Americans would describe it as something like *modest wear;* my mom would find it profane. Somewhere I'm there, in the plastic and polyester.

Dr. Amis held a meeting for staff every morning. He was especially tyrannous that term, due to the vandalism issue.

"More soup," he announced. "This time on my desk. We have our suspicions. The janitorial staff, for one thing. Yes, indeed. Keep eyes out. Keep your eyes aware."

Caroline beside me again, silent laughter. We left the auditorium together to take our posts by the entranceway. Her company was the only thing that made morning duty sufferable, especially in the deadened winter, when students swapped their Yarmulkas for fuzzy hats to hide their Airpods. Caroline was more comfortable with discipline than I was.

"Off," Caroline said. The boy assumed a look of obligatory sheepishness and removed his New York Giants beanie. Grabbed his Yarmulka, jammed it onto his head. Caroline allowed him to pass.

A student bounced toward the school door. "Uh, Jared," I said. "You know you can't wear that inside."

"Please, Miss." he said. "It was a Hannukah gift."

It was a knit hat, with intricate anime characters stitched around the crown. Jared's obsession with anime extended to his schoolwork, where the margins of his homework and essays were cobwebbed with drawings of Ghibli figures and Naruto Uzumaki.

"Sorry, Jared. It's got to come off."

"How about until I'm at my desk, Miss?"

I was aware of Jared's mother watching us from her car, hovering in the drop-off circle. She had sent Jared to school one day with a gift after he'd told her I'd recently moved to town for the teaching job. The internet instructed me to perch it above my doorframe at an angle, that Mezuzahs were used as a sort of spiritual shield for homes. A shield from what? I'd thought. The things that want to break in will break in and get inside me. Jared's mother never asked about it.

Jared stared up at me with his lips in a flat line, eyes all wide. If not for the soppy sadness of his eyes he'd almost exactly resemble The Kaonashi, etched into the wool above his left ear.

"All right," I said. "Till you get to your classroom."

"Thanks, Miss." He rushed in.

"You know someone's going to –" Caroline began before a screech from the innards of the school, the shout of Dr. Amis on a morning cull – "Young man in the cartoons? Take that off immediately."

I took the long way round the school back to my room, to avoid the stench of dill and old chicken emanating from the main hallway. But I could still smell it, the rot and broth and hunger, as I opened my laptop to write a new *Jane Eyre* lesson.

At home that night I lay naked, apart from my head cover, on the bathroom floor. The light in there was the brightest in the apartment, and beneath it the reality of my skin condition entrenched itself. The waxy welts were cylindric with ragged edges, vaguely greenish under my skin, so that they emerged in a befuddled, stormy brown. Other bits of my body felt soft and mealy, as if weak and collapsible at the next minor disturbance. My legs were soft and round, but that was okay, they'd always been, despite plenty of embarrassed time and money sent to fitness gurus and influencers and coaches who promised *your best legs ever!* I smelt something garlicky from my folds, realized I needed a shower.

I thought of what mom would say if she could reach me. Badra, get it together, filthy. Have you no shame?

I've got it in droves, I'd think. Shame in gallons, truckfulls. Shame that would shock you.

Dr. Amis' fury the next morning confirmed our suspicions that the soup thrower was still at large, and that they were bent on whatever point they wanted to make.

"Don't you think it's strange," Caroline said, "That it's always the same type of soup? I heard that it's homemade. Matzoh Ball. Classic."

"A kid's packed lunch. Right?"

"I don't know. You'd think a kid would throw, like, a canned soup."

"I don't know that it's the type of soup that matters to them. Right?"

"Maybe. Did you see the notes about the cultural initiative?"

I had just read it through. "What are you going to bring in?"

"*Harry Potter?*" she said. "I loved that one as a kid?"

"It's hard to tell what Dr. Amis really wants."

"I've talked to four teachers who have already decided on sections from the Torah. Utter kiss-asses. But Dr. Amis will love it."

At home that night I scanned my bookshelf. I imagined my mom, pointing out the collected works of Fadwa Tuqan. Badra, she'd say. You *love* her poems. I tucked Tuqan's collection into my work bag.

The following morning Dr. Amis announced that our submissions for a "representative cultural text" should be in the staff Google Doc by the end of the week. In our prep period, Caroline pulled out *Harry Potter and the Sorcerer's Stone,* wrote a Powerpoint on the ways in which she saw herself in the text.

And where was I? In the painful winter cold? With my mom, in so much terror and hopelessness? In my refusal to take my medication, despite the fact I picked it up every single month? Underneath the Yarmulkas that I was forced to force our pupils to wear? In the barrage of pastel Instagram infographics with statistics and mock shock, which I – for some reason that I could not know – refused to repost myself?

"You okay?" Caroline had stopped clickclacking.

"Yes," I said. "Just deciding on a text to submit."

"Can't go wrong with Torah, if you're unsure."

"No," I said. "That's definitely right."

Naked on the bathroom floor again. Headscarf on. I thought that it might be worth seeking out a dermatologist. The raised welts were bright green and orange. My entire body felt collapsible, soft. Destructible.

And perhaps a therapist, for I was haunted by my own rot. I smelt old broth and celery and dill everywhere. Not just in the streets, in places where I could pretend it was city smells. No – it was within me, wafting from crevices and strengthening with movement. It is all in your head, Badra, mom would say. Your imagination has always been active.

I opened my laptop. The instructions on the Google Doc: *Each teacher will give a three-minute presentation in assembly on a text that represents them. They should connect the text to their culture.*

Fadwa Tuqan's *The Last Melody,* I wrote beside my name. My presentation would fall off my lips like hanging flowers. It would be simple, easy, right, like a song bridge that clicks.

I woke very early the next morning. The mealiness of my skin shocked me, made me afraid to touch myself. I waited for panic to come. It didn't. The anxiety of the cultural presentation, I thought, must be deranging me. Sat up, pulled my laptop out. Jane Austen's *Emma*, I wrote beside my name. Shut the laptop, flicked on a lamp to observe my spongey skin. I suppose I had suspected for a while that I was changing into a matzoh ball. Mom's voice yet again. Change is a good thing, Badra. Embrace it. It made a sort of sense. It also made a sort of sense, to me, when I raised my arm and took a bite.

ONCE ON A CLEAR DAY

The tree was only a tree, if it were only you, or even me, looking at it, albeit a very large and a very old one. And it was coming down. The way that Sheila felt when she heard about the tree's scheduled chop was something like what other people might feel once the airplane is smooth again after that particular kind of threatening turbulence. The tree obstructed her view of the river. And this she believed obstructed everything else, as in, her general welfare, and her productivity levels, and her interest in being alive, and so on. Things could be good, wonderful even, if not for the way that tree protruded across her vision. Her therapist disagreed. This therapist, thought Sheila, was delusional. And anyway, ever since the town had sent out the notice of the planned road and horticultural works for that year, she was perfectly happy.

She was seen and heard on her fast walks down the road and back again, as she hummed melodies she'd dreamt up in the night. Because at last she was dreaming again. The tunes had lyrics to them now, and she realized that – for the first time in a long time – she thought she felt God in music once more, like she had when she was a girl.

"The tree comes down," she would sing. "And the view of the river rips right on open." There were other renditions of this song, but they all alluded to the fact that once the tree came down, Sheila would be able to see all of the Hudson River and beyond, right from her living room window. And on sunny days, even Manhattan. She would be able to distinguish the Empire State Building all the way out there. And that was what success felt like to her.

On the day before the tree was set to come down, Sheila spoke to Jen on the phone. She sat in the living room and gazed across the road. Its tendrils waved offensively.

"See, Jen, once the tree is down the whole sky will open up. Sky like you've never seen it before."

"The sky is still up there," Jen pointed out, "Even though the tree obstructs your view of it."

"It may as well not be. While the tree stands, I couldn't tell you the color of the sky. I'd be unable to tell you, Jen, if even it was a clear day out."

"Well," Jen said, "The sky is clear today. No clouds."

"And starting tomorrow I will be able to see for myself, thank you, Jen."

"Don't you feel a sense of attachment to the tree, a little?"

"There are trees *everywhere*, Jen. I could go out to the trails and see as many as I want anytime. It's that one that I want down."

"I dunno," said Jen. "I like the sense of nature that it instills on the block. And my daughter likes it under there."

"Jen, I'm as into nature as the next. I could talk trees all day if you wanted. But *that* tree never spoke to me. It just never did."

"Okay. Bye, Sheil—"

Sheila's daydreams came back and reminded her of the coming foliage destruction and all of the things that she might see, soon, *finally,* in the nothingness of sky above her head. When she put the phone down, Jen looked out at the willow through her kitchen window. It was the tallest of its kind in the county, and it occasionally attracted hipster tourism. Young people from the city came to wrap their arms around its colossal trunk, post a photo on their feed: *tree hugger*. And families picnicked beneath the weeping willow, whose tentacles formed a circle so broad and dense that you could spend a whole afternoon in its shade and think you were completely alone, even if somebody watched you from just over there. Jen thought of her daughter, who liked to sit beneath the tree and scroll on social media between the end of school and dinner time. She looked out the window and waited for Eve to come home.

At school, Eve could not look at anybody in the cafeteria, because they were all looking at her.

"Everybody has seen them," Eve whispered. "Literally everybody has seen my bare tits and everything."

"I heard from Trip that it was Jordan's mistake," Sarah answered. "He accidentally took a screenshot and it got picked up by the cloud or something, and he has public pages on his cloud? Which the whole team has access to? Cause it has their plays on it?"

Eve felt brutalized all day, though nobody had touched her. It was in their giggling superiority. The worst thing that a girl could be in that school was a slut. Yet Eve felt she'd been worse before. She'd been stupid on exams and she'd been harsh and violently temperamental toward her mother. She'd snuck out and become a woman by giving a hand job in the backseat of a car that was parked solemnly in the Dunkin' Dunkins lot. She'd spread false rumors about her friends for no real reason. But none of that will be my downfall, she thought. It'll be that I'm a slut.

During free period she found Trip amongst the rest of the team, all huddled around a red table in the library. She had never spoken to most of those boys before, never even looked them dead on. But Trip was different. The one thing that Eve had always wanted was to be somehow special.

Also, she wanted to be adored. To be adored by somebody special – the quarterback and cutest boy in school who came from a good family who was dedicated to attending church – had felt briefly like life was the best it could be and would ever be again. And he'd written back in the messages section of the app, *you're so sexy for a freshman lol,* and she'd said, *want to see more?* because she wanted more of everything he said and did and thought.

"Hi?"

Trip looked at a spot on the wall behind her head as the boys clapped him on the back and chortled and contorted themselves into suggestive positions. The air around her felt choked by whispers, and they all said *slut slut slut.*

"Yeah?"

"Can we talk?"

"We can message later again if you want," he responded, and this was uproarious to the other boys.

She'd never known real mortification. It felt like physical pain, like something in her stomach had split. She tried to keep composed as she left, and then she darted away toward the girls' room. She sent a text to her mom which said, I don't feel well at all, please could you call the school and tell them that I've been throwing up in the bathroom and have permission to go home?

When her mom didn't answer for several minutes, she abandoned that effort and ran out a side door of the building. She wound up on a quiet street behind the school. She pulled out her phone and started for home.

Other people had also seen the images on the cloud, but not all of them were in the school building that day. The Scarstown School District Board of Education met in a historic mansion on the hill just beyond the high school. At present they gazed in shock upon the blown-up image of the freshman girl, who'd bared her whole-entire-everything to a boy on the football team through an app. Some of the men in the room, all of whom were fathers of students at the school, didn't really know where to look. It was objectively fascinating, surely. Who among us isn't just a tiny bit curious? One of the men looked straight at a single pixel until it was indiscernible, and the whole image turned to abstraction. The women who sat around the conference table consumed the image in its entirety, knotting up their lips in academic and inquisitive study.

Lena Candy couldn't believe what she was looking at. "I find this incredibly whoreish," she said. "I mean wholly inappropriate for our boys. Should we all just fund their porn subscriptions now instead?"

"It's a valid point," agreed Peter. "I'm inclined to agree."

"It's a circus, what these girls do. It's a circus. Do we really want our institutions of learning to become circuses which harbor such whoreish girls?"

"I really don't think so," said Peter.

"This is what kids do," interjected a different father. "Everybody does it. All of them. Is it really about this one issue? And who else was even involved?"

He opened up a new tab which accessed the page's history. His mouse moved across the PC, which was projected hugely on the far wall of the conference room. Soon the screen displayed every change that had ever been made to the document, and whose account those changes belonged to. "See," he said. "We can actually see who originally posted the photo."

"It's a fiasco," shrieked Lena. "Turn it off. It's child

pornography. Close your eyes. Turn them downward. We could be arraigned for even looking."

Peter and some of the women looked in other directions.

"Look at all of these motions," Lena said. She gestured across the broad conference table. "Just Look at how much we have to get through. We have to work harder."

"What's the next motion then?" somebody called.

"The willow on maple is coming down tomorrow. It's a known spot for deviants. It's highly promiscuous. Children go there to drink and take drugs, and other things. It's a hideaway for local reprobates and a risk to our community. It needs to come down. We have received written permission from almost everybody who lives in the vicinity. We did not get permission from the woman, Jen, who lives next door. But the majority rules in horticultural and education matters, as the town edict lays out."

School Board meetings usually devolved into Lena's personal orations. Lena would've liked to have been born a man so that she could've become a legitimate pastor within her church. She enjoyed the process of preaching, from practicing her speech as she fell asleep to articulating it with devasting clarity before the board. And she liked the feeling of advocating for things.

"Think of our children," she continued. "They are our only future."

"What do you mean by our only future, exactly?" someone asked.

"It's rhetoric."

"It's time to call it," said Peter. "All motions approved. Nice work everyone."

Everybody left. They wandered around to source lunch and then went about their usual work of sitting at home.

As she walked home, Lena passed a girl who looked like she should've been at school. Cutting class? Doing drugs? Sex? Lena almost stepped toward her to open an enquiry, but the girl was quickly off, and her head had been angled toward her phone, so she'd not had a good look at her.

Eve didn't notice anybody as she walked home, because she was skipping nervously through the school's cloud pages. Her phone kept dropping WiFi and didn't load anything until she was beneath the safety of her weeping willow tree, where she lay down and brought her phone so close that it touched the tip of her nose. When she found the picture of herself, she was shocked at what she looked like. That doesn't even look like me, she said to the tree. That girl looks like a slut.

And later that night she made loud vomiting sounds from the bathroom, so that her mom would insist that she stay home from school the next day.

Trip Candy's house was also full of noise that night, because his mother was in a rage. She'd grabbed his phone and hurled it into the living room wall. All of its components flung in opposite directions, and she grabbed those too, and flung them toward Trip with fast precision. And then on her own phone she pulled up the photo and shoved it into her son's face. See? Lena said. See? See? See? See this whore, this slut? See the thing that will cause your fall?

Neither Trip nor Eve were in school the next day, which the student body found entertaining. That's mortifying, it was whispered. If you're going to do it, at least own up to it, right? Like, why be a slut in private?

And Eve was convinced that she was, indeed, a slut. She sat underneath her tree again as she evaded school, wondered how she'd gone from a girl to a high schooler and then a whore so fast. She'd wanted to be a lot of other things in her life, but right now it seemed like this was what she was and all she'd ever be. She heard soft singing from beyond the willow's curtain.

"The tree's soon dead," Sheila sang. "The sunset's red, the view will fill my head with the happiest sights."

Sheila traced the tree's circumference in soft footsteps, over and over and over again. Who could blame me? she thought. It's a demented plant.

Then Sheila heard the sounds of official voices nearby, and stopped to watch the Board of Education give instructions to a crew of tree surgeons. She heard the fresh BRRRRRR and the WEERRRRRRR and the BUZZZZZ of a chainsaw from a great height. It sounded like an orchestra.

Sheila's stomach atomized as the first branch was cut. Then her spirit lifted higher as the floating surgeon slowly cut throw the tree's curtain, tendril by winding tendril.

Lena Candy watched from the sidewalk, surrounded by the rest of the Board. "This is a great thing for our kids," she said. "We should all be proud of the work we've done here."

"Is that a child?" someone called out. The surgeon continued his dignified work and tendrils fell and landed at their feet. A girl looked out to them through the falling branches and turned her phone in their direction.

WORK TRIP

In the Middle of the United States there is corn. And less ubiquitous, flowers. I drive through Kansas, the middlest of the middle, and its middleness mocks and bites, as does all of the corn. It has husks that arch to steroidal heights. But amongst the corn there are sunflowers, here there is a set of five, the fifth one bowed against the sky.

The drive through Kansas is so predictable that the throughway signage is moot. There are no exits and no alternate directions besides onward. Right now, Kansas feels encased in a metal of its own design, and the corn stalks are stolid bars between me and everywhere else.

In a McDonald's at a truck stop I order a diet coke and the fizz of it floats up my nose. Classical music plays throughout the seating section, piano sparkles. I sit in a booth beside the neon children's play area. I did not realize that McDonald's still had those anywhere in the country – this one even has a ball pit, all primary colors. A mother watches her toddler dive about in it. She takes off her shoes and socks and dips her toes into the ball pit slowly, as if checking a pool's temperature. And then she retracts her toes and puts her sock back on. The music fades and a radio announcer's voice breaks through, thanks us for listening to Classical 57 in Finney County. We've got a long day of classics and some deep cuts for you, he says. But first he has to hand us over to his colleague who will tell us about the traffic situation. The new announcer talks about a jam somewhere and clear skies and goes on for a bit about highway vigilance. The mother scoops the toddler from the ball pool and he throws a fit, screaming and going red then blue. I vaguely worry that he might choke himself but the mother seems unconcerned, takes his hand and leads him to the parking lot.

Back on the road the radio has turned to static. Not even Classical 57, which has been clear eyed for the last hundred miles, reaches me anymore. The farmlands on both sides of the highway remind me of deep dark woods from a children's story. The sunflower and corn stalks are so high, and they flash by in alternating patches. In the way back distance of these fields are sprawling complexes, which I know are a part of the farming industrial machine of the country, because I've just read that book by Michael Pollen, which all of the girls at home described as one of this year's must-reads. A reporter manages to break through the static of Classical 57 as he laments the recent anniversary of The Clutters. I feel a suddenly desperate urge to pee, which is something that I should've considered before the large diet coke at McDonald's. I pull onto the shoulder, thinking that that's barely necessary – I've not seen another car for hours.

Flowers and people tend not to look too much alike under ordinary circumstances. But under circumstances that are so terribly ordinary that they incarcerate the mind in deadness –extreme tedium so rare that it hits you like asthma – flowers and people can start to look remarkably similar. Which is what I think now as I squat behind the car and start to dribble, and a particular sunflower at the edge of the road has no petals but a human face. And I see that the face is attached to a long human body, which belongs to a girl.

She doesn't seem to notice that I'm mid-squat. I fumble around with my underwear and pull them up, and my jeans. It's messy and I'm annoyed by the damp bits of fabric when she calls,

Hey there!

Edification as I rise from my squat. She must be some kind of a farm girl; this is her parents' land. Although I can't see her very clearly amongst the flowers I imagine that she's freckled from long hours under the sun. As she steps out I see that I'm probably right – she's in grayish dungarees which are muddy around the ankles. She lifts her hand and smiles, so I go closer.

And I think about next weekend. I think about the girls all gathered at Cracked Egg. They'll ask about this road trip, expecting something of the same as ever. I was put in a shitty hotel room with a view of nothing much, and work comped everything, as usual, but I chose to eat at predominantly McDonaldses, as usual, and there was the presentation of slides which people congratulated me over. But this time I could tell the story of an ephemeral relationship, an act of kindness beyond their capacities. I could illustrate my overt friendliness and my adventurism, but also note that I, unlike them, have found a certain beauty in middle America. I have wrenched free of their urbanity and sought meaning in places where they aren't even bothered to look. No wonder you collect bits of boyish men off dating apps and wonder why you're so unhappy, I'd imply. No wonder everything about you is so overtaken by malaise.

I've realized that it's actually not too bad out there, I could say. In fact outside of our little shared places, life is still happening and people are still working and they are still feeling happy. In fact, the folk are extremely friendly and I befriended one. Believe it or not. And this storytelling moment will suggest that I myself am also well and good, and that the empty purposelessness that has overtaken them is no match for me, not yet. I know that they believe that the deep dark nothing has entered and consumed me, too, but girls – I'd say –wait until you hear about this farm girl that I befriended out in Kansas.

And it's like she understands that I've come to this decision, because she leaps over now to the backseat door, which is unlocked. I realize that I never lock those, and wonder if that might be dangerous. I've barely got a foot in the car before she leaps in and crashes the door closed. She says,

Thank you! Thank you so much!

I look at her through my rearview as I turn out of the shoulder and realize that she is fully a woman, no girl and no teenager. I am tickled by a bitter thought that's been nagging me lately, which is that I, too, am no teenager and certainly no girl, and yet I tend to despise other grown women, purely for not being young anymore. I decide that this act of kindness will be the start of my redemption arc.

I see that she is freckled, so about one thing I was right.

I ask where she's headed. She says,

Anywhere. And you? Where are you going?

And I almost tell her, except I don't want her to think I'm another consultant passing through with no intention to get to the know the place or its inhabitants. So I say, Uh, just going home.

She goes silent for a long time. Somewhere in that silence I say again, Where do you want to be dropped off? and I also try to think of conversation starters that might make two middle-aged women form an unlikely but raucous and fulfilling friendship. My mind feels wholly empty of ideas, like I've never started a real conversation before now.

So then there is just silence. It waits there, as if expecting one of us to do something particular. We don't – we just sit there and water the silence. I'm watching her through the rearview mirror in a way that I think might appear furtive. She is looking keenly out the window now. This plan, I think, is ridiculous – am I an idiot? I scan the upcoming road signs for an exit, thinking that I'll wish her well, but tell her that I've gone as far as I'll be going today. For the first time in ages, I pay attention to the road signs, hoping for a yellow neon M or a truck stop symbol. Instead I see a green billboard appear from the metal fields of the ants and the petals and the corn: Kansas State Penitentiary, Do Not Pick Up Hitchhi-

The girl smiles, it smothers half her body.

I wish now that she were a flower.

NIMROD COMMISSION

It is always unclear which comes first: the music or the motive. Did I listen to the blues because I was so blue, or was I so blue because I only listened to the blues, and I repeated their pain and drudgery over and over and over again through my headphones?

Now it doesn't matter, if it ever did. That year I went to their bluish corner and told them about my blues and that alone felt right, and then the musicians, they felt sorry for me and they offered me a job. They thought, *we've got to help her get out of that sorority house.* No – actually, what happened – I went to the careers center and I nagged a receptionist to schedule an appointment, during which I begged for a summer internship. I didn't care how menial, how repetitive, how undesirable. I said, just get me out of here for a few months, please. Well, we've got a lot of roles in D.C., the careers counsellor said.

So on a blue February morning of that blue winter I grabbed a blue Kappa Alpha pen from my backpack and signed my name to the civil services summer internship placement program form, and I rode to D.C. in a desperate blue Greyhound, and on the way there I changed it up and listened to bluegrass. I blew away, because D.C. was supposed to be my summertime distraction, so that was my attempt at something new.

I did start seeing new colors out there, at least for the first week. But then I began to suspect that maybe location didn't have much to do with it at all, and that the things that pestered me might be caught in my memory instead.

My immediate supervisor was Kevin Burns. Burns was a ginormous man. Both his body and his voice swelled to exponential heights everywhere he went. Here's how I met him:

"Summer intern? I want you to know something extremely important about working for the EEOC," he said.

He always pranced around as he spoke. He was a level 14 government employee, and that's out of 15. Nobody seemed to know who the number 15 of the EEOC was, which meant that Burns had the best office in the whole commission. Which isn't saying much. The EEOC occupied one floor of a brutalist cube building, which sat at the edge of the city. On that first day I'd been invited to tour the building, and had waited around for somebody to come get me before I realized that this tour was a solo thing. I walked around the other floors – we were below Alcohol & Firearms and above Housing. As I climbed upward, color drained out in increments.

Other students who'd got their civil services applications in earlier were all up at capitol hill and the courts, surrounded by white marble, which looked pretty and professional in the backgrounds of their new headshots. Burns didn't care about any of that. He talked a lot about how he had ADHD and OCD – "but I'm really anti-neurological medication" – and so he hired a cleaner for his office weekly.

He repeated himself as I sat across from him.

"Sorry? Uh- sir?"

"Who the fuck?"

So I laughed at that, right. This was May twenty-eighth and it was my first earnest laugh of the month. There is a contagious disease out there right now – a sense-of-humor deficiency. With humor as a hot commodity, I thought it best to laugh whenever I could.

Burns had no deficiency in humor. He simply did not find this funny.

"Shut up. You're being hysterical. I am not a sir. I'm a Burns."

He spoke with his eyebrows as well as his mouth and looked at me like I mattered, while he and I both knew that I didn't matter much at all, in any way that you might measure it.

"This Department does extremely important work for the United States. For the disadvantaged. Have you heard of the *disadvantaged?* They are running rampant across this country. But we don't protect the young. Don't forget. We protect against the *discriminated.* Understand?"

It was the young that so depressed him; they had nothing to offer beyond pathetic attempts to change the trajectory of things. Everybody was agreed that this century was downward-looking. But the young only ever looked *up,* he would say. Their optimism will eat them, he'd lament, as he led the morning meeting. Optimism will literally eat them like a virus for which there is no vaccine. He found this very funny.

He pointed at a calendar on the wall behind his desk, marked up with A's and B's and C's, and phrases like ON SITE VISIT or INTAKE DAY.

"This is my schedule."

"Right."

"It is very full."

A pause, during which I pretended to consider this new information.

"Interns are expected to enable this functioning Commission to remain a functioning Commission. I have stridently ensured its functioning. You will not dismember it."

"Of course."

"The most important day of the week is—" He slapped the calendar with one hand, and I looked at his fingertips, which points to some mangled letters.

"Wednesday. Communal Coffee Wednesday," Burns said. "The way to rise in this commission, even to stay in this commission, is to never forget your assigned Wednesday. Because we run on schedule. Yes?"

"Sorry. Does that mean something that I don't really understand yet?"

Kevin Burns laughed. He laughed and laughed and hooted once or twice.

He laughed for so long that I started reading the titles of the books on the shelves behind his desk:

Common Sense. History Of The Decline And Fall Of the Roman Empire. Elvis's Favorite Recipes: A Three Step Guide. King James's Bible—

"Enlighten me," said Burns. "There's nothing hidden in code about Communal Coffee Wednesdays. Do you think this is a joke? *Do* you? Because if you do – you won't last, girl—"

"I didn't mean to joke."

"Wednesdays are vital to our operation. Every Commission employee, including unpaid interns" – he raised his eyebrows at me here, as though I'd forgotten who I was – "Are assigned a Communal Coffee Wednesday. There are some employees around here that only bring along coffee on their Coffee day."

He closed his eyes and moaned a little, with a flash of tongue.

"Do *you* want to be the type of batshit employee that only brings along coffee for their Coffee Wednesday? Coffee and some milk and sugar?"

"No. I don't think so."

"Stunning. I reward effort. There are certain unwritten rules around here. I would know. I'm rewriting an account of my own personal history in novel form. And I've rewritten a recent history of the EEOC several times throughout my tenure. I know a thing about the unwritten, girl. Just don't be a moron. I mean *donuts*."

"Donuts to go with the coffee," I realized.

"This is a nether corner of D.C. It's a shithole. People might attempt to convince you that it's a nice area. They may use phrases like *up-and-coming*. But it is a wasteland."

"Alright," I said. "Makes sense."

"I thought it might. However, it does have one redeeming feature. There's a Dunkin' Donuts, on the corner. Understand? There just isn't really any time for you not to understand, so."

"Yes."

There was another slap on the calendar.

"If you fail on your assigned Communal Coffee Wednesday, I will find you incompetent, and unfit to work for our American government."

"Is that – okay. Is that about all there is to know?

"Well go on to HR and fill out your forms and take a desk in the communal interns' room. There will be a landline on your desk but its only connection is me. So if it rings, pick up."

He tossed me a few unmarked yellow files. "Read these. Determine grounds or not for discrimination. You can't spend more than ten minutes on your initial read through of each case. There isn't any time."

He pulled a file marked A from a binder and flicked through it.

"Should I just get to work now, then?"

"If you must. Tell the other interns – what are their names? Just tell them what I said about the cases, and about communal coffee Wednesdays. I cannot have these dire meetings with each and every one of them. There just isn't any time."

"I'll tell them. But I think there's only one in the same role as me. I think she's called India."

"I don't wholly care. Just tell her about the cases and the Wednesdays."

"Alright, then. Thanks."

"Goodbye, goodbye," and he turned away to start on another document, so I went out to the interns' room and chose a desk in a corner, where I thought I'd be unnoticed.

Oh, he was out of his mind – but I felt such affinity for him after that first meeting. Such connectedness and closeness and even idolatry. I'd spent a year in a depression of my own design. And here was somebody even more mental than I was. I thought that he was wonderful.

As I turned back to shut his office door I saw him write a thick black C on a folder and toss it into the metal waste bin beside his desk. He threw a Three Musketeers wrapper in after it. And it seemed, to me, that it was all the same, really. So I left and cocooned into my desk and turned on my headphones and spent the rest of the day on deliberations over what I'd listen to on the way back home again.

The Capitol is split into neighborhoods. It is not a casual or a cordial separation. You stay in your neighborhood and your neighborhood stays in you. But everybody together, no matter what type of material you built your house from or how pure your dog's parentage, was on the lookout for distraction from the suffocating doldrums of American summer. The literary types who read new-wave poetry and Penguin Classics, they sloped around Dupont Circle and carried metabolic tea for lovers and exes but themselves most of all. Looked for allegory everywhere. Summertime was made for people like that, people like you: the lucky, the gentle.

But life in D.C. felt hoarded elsewhere by others, and whoever they were, they were getting greedy. Leroy Carr understood that – that aching nothing, and nobody to do it with. In place of life there were office tasks, which became this horror party of case files: discrimination complaints. I cannot, and will not, tell you any details. And not because I am legally and morally obliged not to. I couldn't tell you about any of the cases because I did not read them.

On the very last page of each yellow file, there was a list of options, one of which I was to check. That check mark indicated my idea of where the case file should go next, according to my discerning analysis.

Here is what I did, every day, till the weeks deflated together into one deadpan season. I placed a black CHECK on the point that read, "C: CLOSE CASE." I sent it toward its merry catastrophe. I felt in terrible disrepair but the lovely music helped, and to that soundscape I closed hundreds and hundreds of filed cases.

I got a call from Burns, come straight to my office, he said. It was urgent.

He was sat behind his desk, both elbows perched and supporting his face, upon which his mouth looked plastered into pavement. Two weeks prior he'd given up on the writing of both his newest personal history and a detailed analysis of the commission's inner workings of the last decade. This had put him in a bad mood and he'd become petty, blasting into rages if somebody brought in the wrong donut holes or tried to swap one coffee keg for decaf, or if anybody put a case forward to further investigation. I didn't do any of those things, so I usually went unnoticed, until I sat before him in the office.

"Yes?"

"You are running absolutely excellent numbers," he said. He nodded toward a wire basket labeled "C" to his right. It looked a landfill itself, that's how wide it burst with pages.

"I mean, that is a deplorable degree of apathy," he went on. "Where did you learn how to be so good?"

"Thanks," I said. "It's second nature."

"I've never seen anything like it," he said. "And I've been trying so long."

"I just don't think many of the cases warrant much more."

"But of course they don't," he shrieked, and then the grim lips morphed into this

hysterical grin, which I'd never seen on him before.

"Warrant? *Warrant?* These cases have never warranted. And they never will. But you get it. You *understand* the mission of my Commission. You just don't care, do you?"

I did not.

"I do," I said.

He looked at me like he saw me. I might have moved him, emotionally.

"Thank you," he said. "For your commitment."

"That's okay," I said. "Happy to help." As I left I felt a strange reverent urge to bow.

I was the commission's most productive intern that summer.

By the fifth week I'd turned over two hundred cases, and I'd listened to so many new albums and deep cuts that I was back to the beginning again with Muddy Waters. He sang a lot about being nowhere, so much in fact that it made you feel you might be somewhere. There were worried notes, which is a type that falls just above or below the regular major or minor on the scale. It's off, so it makes you feel you've left the oven on. It's a very beautiful worry.

I shot down those two hundred cases because they were all at varied levels of unimportance, none of them with litigious potential. Or so I imagined would be the case, if I'd ever cared to look. I filled America's communal, stinking wastelands with yellow cases and the wasted time of the good citizens who'd filed them.

Rock n' roll.

The trouble was that a certain blues note was often the most economical means of establishing whether or not I was still alive. So I tried to find it everywhere. I created a skilled drumline solo from the rapidity and reliability of my pen hitting C, C, C, C, -- and eventually it became like music to me.

India liked to interrupt my goings on.

She was seventeen, a high school senior on an extracurricular project. Yes – I may not have been the voice for the common good. I might've practiced discretionary omniscience with a heavy hand in my work habits. But anything – *anything* – murderer, pedophile, cannibal, arsonist – anything is better than being an American teenager.

India was tall and skinny but in sort of remorseful way, like she wished that so much of her didn't exist. And she had this oval face, long, with pokey lips and wet eyes, and curly hair that clung to everything. And every time she looked at you it was out of sympathy, like she was sad for you, but the fact is she was just sad for herself, and just wanted to pretend.

"What are you *workin'* on?" she asked. She came from Sandcastle, Pennsylvania, but when asked, she only said that she was from PA. And she had this habit of dropping her *g*'s, as if they embarrassed her.

"I'm writing a Pre-Interview notice to a Complaint Filer," I told her.

"Oh, wow," she said. "What are their grounds?"

She liked that word: *grounds*. It didn't sound idiotic, and it was often the case that there were too much or too little of them, and someone always needed *some* grounds or lack thereof. When India first heard Mr. Burns use the word *grounds,* she folded it up into a wrinkle in her brain as the most useful word in all the office.

"They don't have any grounds," I told her. "That's why I'm writing them a Pre-Interview notice."

She looked at me like I'd morphed into a preacher. I looked at my computer screen, and then at a hangnail on my thumb, and then at the grey carpet, for so long that it turned almost blue. After I'd looked at everything besides India, and even closed my own eyes for a second, I relented and looked back at her.

"Because I'm going to close the case," I said. "Since they don't have any grounds. And you've got to send them a notice beforehand. It's their right. You can't terminate a grievance until they know that that's your intention."

"Their right," she said. Dreamy now, like she thought about individual rights to put herself to bed, starry: *rights, rights, rights,* like a lullaby, and she tucked that word into a special wrinkle in her brain too. "Good for you," she said. "Preservin' their rights."

She paused and then looked back at the space between our desks, as if there was something still left to say.

"Alright," I said. "Thanks."

The Equal Employment Opportunity Commission is still around, in some form, though I hear they've moved to a Capitol Hill building, which means that somebody started taking it seriously.

But I'll tell you what it was when I was there: It was a commission of nimrods.

Around the end of June, it was all Delta Blues, that really mournful deep Southern kind which moves you so forcefully that you wonder if you even have a right to be wrecked by it like that, what with having privilege. But I figured that my time in Michigan and in that house had been its own kind of hellscape and that that counted for something, gave me a right to be sad and tortured and allowed me to cry. And anyway it's music, it's *music.* If the land of the free means anything to me, it's in the proliferation of its streaming apps.

I operated at my best – and by that I mean that there were more bits of me present than there were missing – in the real heart of the Blues, and there was Robert Johnson and he was Walking Side By Wide With The Devil, and then he talked of how he would beat his woman until satisfaction, according to him. Like anybody else I found the song uncomfortable by modern standards. But you try and listen to it without being wrecked by how pretty.

It was my metro music. In the morning rush to work I'd listen to my music and try to determine the titles of other people's books. Everybody was reading non-fiction or fantasy with bad covers. So I'd think, how pathetic, and embarrassing. The music would always be better than shitty essay collections and sexy fairies. Then I'd get off at the metro station and the silence would come to me again.

I lied earlier. There was one case that I did read. As a rule I did not interview anybody on the designated public intake days, but India slipped up on her schedule once, and I had to cover. That's how I got landed with a woman in Intake Room F. The yellow file that corresponded with her complaint sat unopened and unmarked atop my desk.

She looked haggard in that particular way that has to do with the area under the eyes. Purple from sleep deficiency and deep, almost like I could look right through them and peak out the back of her brain. I sat her across from me, told her about the procedure. We go from here to there to here. And then we send it off again to them. And then they'll decide to do with it. She looked only vaguely in my direction.

"Would you describe the grievance," I said.

I'm obligated not to reveal details, but I can tell you the first bit of her response, and it was this:

"So I've been, uh, I think, the word for it would be harassed, at work – by my manager."

Horror story, horror story. And Kevin Burns started writing a new novel this morning, then got sick in the staff bathroom from overeating sweets again. India has a Boy Crush at the high school. Record high temperatures yesterday. I positioned my pen on C - CLOSE CASE, and I thought about the soundtrack to the rest of the afternoon.

You can't watch the news these days without this kind of story popping up and interrupting. You might wonder about the government's dealings in it – Have they got days set aside for that, time slots? Do they line up all the abused, strip them down like soldiers, whip out a ruler, a protractor, offer them a tea, a coffee, make yourselves at home! Is there ever any small talk before the retreat to misery? What sort of music did you listen to on the way over?

None of that, not really.

"Where do you work?" I asked, as a formality. Certain parts of the form had to be completed in order to officially close the case. How many times, I asked, and of what nature. Have you complained, and to whom? Would you describe it as pervasive and/or debilitating?

"Pretty, uh, regularly," she answered. "I don't really know what to do anymore because I have two kids, and it's difficult for me to go to work but of course I have to, and I have tried to complain but the thing is I'm actually just a new teacher, I'm still training? So I don't have my certification, and they're giving it to me for free, because I'm doing coursework and teaching a full schedule? But I need the certification to, you know, get a better job? So I can't leave. And I also can't get fired. And I don't know who does the firing. But I think it's him. I don't know who I would complain to – it's my immediate boss and also the school vice principal, so it's like—"

This was as familiar as any old fairytale, but much less entertaining. And the ending was always the *same*, wasn't it, with all of it.

"Can I have the location of the school?" I asked. "And your department?" The file was becoming ripe with information, which meant that I could place it directly into Burns' "C" basket and close it that day.

"It's the performing arts school in Dupont Circle," she said. "The Bell School of Music and Theatre. I'm in music. I do whatever the other teachers don't have time for. So, like, keyboard lessons, a lot of the time. But I'm going to teach jazz when I'm certified."

I put down my pen and looked at her in order to see her, rather than just to look, if you get me.

Here's what I did with that case and that case only that summer: I checked the box marked "A" –

"ASSUME INVESTIGATION. PLAUSIBLE LITIGIOUS OPPORTUNITY." And I placed it into its proper basket.

"We'll be in touch," I told her. "I'll walk you out."

She left and the ensuing silence mocked, and I looked out through the window and saw the sidewalk doldrums unchanged, and I thought how fascinating it could all be if only I was somebody else.

On the Wednesday after I'd taken on purple eyes' case, Burns went to the treats table in the break room. It was India's rotation, and her mother had purchased the donuts, walked her to the front door, and given her a kiss on the cheek. I saw the whole thing because I'd hopped off the Metro around the same time.

I went to get a coffee about the same time Burns made his hourly trip. I watched him take the Dunkin' box from the table and retreat with it. I sat some minutes in the intern room again, listened to India pretend to understand the application of statute, then retreated myself into this dull headspace in which nothing much happens. Then Burns rang me up on my fake landline phone and told me to report, so I did, at which point I found him at his desk in confused turmoil. The donuts had felt the worst of his emotion – nine of them had been gutted of their jelly centers. He had started on the surrounding fried dough by the time I got to his office.

"Sit," he said, and licked a finger.

I knew better than to respond.

"Do you think that you're God?" he asked.

"No. I mean, what? Of course not."

"Excellent. Because you are not God. You are an intern. Do you have any idea how disparate that is from being God or even a God amongst many?"

I nodded. I saw that he gripped a yellow file on which I recognized my own handwriting, "A"

"Now that that's settled," he went on, "Why are you taking on cases for investigation? Sending grievances almost directly to litigation? What poor soul has so moved you to this insanity?"

"Mr. Burns," I said, "This could have legitimate legal grounds. It's pervasive harassment. With sexual touching. And I've thrown away hundreds of cases. This is my only A so far."

"And?"

"Could I not at least go to the school, see what's going on – I think there's flaws with internal reporting procedures, and all that. So that's immediate grounds to Request Further Information. Right?"

"An ethos of litigiousness is not something that the commission upholds under my direction. We prefer mediation, verbal and civil conflict resolution. Conversation and agreement. Do you have any idea what our budget is like? And I have taught you about the pitfalls of federal over-interference. I have *taught* you the importance of our purpose, and the treachery of abandoning it. What, exactly, does this woman have to say about her discrimination? Enlighten me."

"It's an immediate supervisor to a subordinate. And it's a private school, so they don't work like any typical school here in the city. They don't have human resources, really, or they have teachers who just act in those roles as volunteers. And there's a disparity in treatment. Over training opportunities and placement. But if I went to the school I could bring you back all of that, I could record it properly."

"You'll have to do one better than a *school,* girl. Schools? Do you have any idea what school staff see these days? Day-in, day-out? All for the pursuit of a clear conscious? She works long hours as a babysitter. Her students can't read. It's degrading. Does she herself have small children? Of course she has small children. She worries about them. So she thinks about all the things she could be doing instead of whatever the fuck it is she does there – what is it again, a music shop?"

"A music school."

"Exactly. No money in it. And they hear of us and they think: *get rich quick*. But Stella, it's all shit. It's cow shit. Delusion. It's crystal clear to me you're dealing with a woman that has endeavored on a sparkling litigious opportunity. This is what's happened. She listens to the horrendous sounds of children on violins. This happens every day, for hours at a time. And when they're not on the violin they're on the trumpet, choking on their reeds and their saliva. This would drive anybody to madness. I sympathize, I do. I would not put it upon myself, no. Not voluntarily. But there she is, listening to horrible, horrible music, and she thinks, I'm wasting away! I could be out, as alive as anybody else. But this, she thinks, is killing me slowly. She comes to innocent girls like you. And you, with your maternal instincts and your biological compassion for members of your own sex – you bite."

"But what if there is something to it? What if it goes up the whole system, your name stamped on the next big case, heard by the Supreme Court? Couldn't you become, like, the people's icon?"

He put his head on his desk.

"I'm sad," he said. "I am sad. You've misread things so deeply."

"The Supreme Court," he sighed. "The people's icon. You used to be so good. I really had vision for you. But you're on a spiral of mental disarray and gross opportune. They've snared you already. You're lost.

"Go to Dupont Circle," he said. "I will entertain this in order to teach you a lesson. And then...yes. The Supreme fucking Court really gives a shit."

"Thank you, Mr. Burns. I appreciate – "

"*Go,*" and he used that booming tone that made it

sound like there were more people in the room than just us, and so I went.

Out in Dupont Circle people wander about at all hours of the day, but nobody seems to have much urgency. They are dressed pristinely, in sets that match and shoes with platforms. It was a hot and beautiful day. Summer was really on us now.

As I walked I felt money and beauty from the Georgetown townhouses trickling down and crawling about. The people out there distract themselves with psychotherapy and mini versions of animals and many long years of rest. If I ever have any money, I'll look into it for myself.

The school was red brick and it looked like somewhere you'd really want to go hear some music, sort of historical but something modern there too.

I watched it from across the street and it watched me back. I realized then what was off about Dupont. Silence, pure and doomed, nobody talking or humming or whistling. You could barely hear the sounds of people thinking.

I considered stopping for a drink because I was alone. I said something in my head that I'd recently started to say aloud. I have yet to break this habit. It puts people off me, especially now that I'm no longer very young.

Hello? I asked.

It is very lonely in here, and it is awfully dark. Hello? Hello?

No-one answered. They usually don't.

The only place to go now, really, was through the main entrance. I rang a notice bell and waited for reception to let me in. In the front office I showed my federal badge and said that I was there for research purposes on behalf of my supervisor, the head of the Equal Employment Opportunity Commission. Might I sit down?

They couldn't actually say no, because we had a notice that elevated us to certain privileges. But by this point in the life of an EEOC complaint, the accused will have taken certain protective measures. I'd wanted to meet the vice principal, but he'd surely been warned to stay away. I couldn't wander freely around the school, looking for just anybody. I had to stay in that glass receptionist office, and speak to whoever was available and willing. The receptionist side eyed me as I showed her my Request for Information. I said, "Could I ask you a few questions? It shouldn't really take long." She sighed, long and deep.

"Okay. How long have you worked here and what's your job title?" I started.

"Two weeks. Trainee office manager."

"Oh. Okay. Right."

In the following silence I became suddenly very aware of the fact that she was much older than me and that really, in so many ways, I still saw myself as just a girl. I still felt so young and stupid and out-of-normal-life. And she was an adult, a fully formed one. I couldn't remember any more of my questions. The longer the silence lasted the harder she looked at me. I knew that she knew exactly what was happening. I'm just a girl pretending.

"Okay. Right," I said again. "Well, is there anyone else that's, maybe, been here a little longer?"

"They're all working at the moment," she said.

"Yeah. No, of course. Okay."

"Sorry," she said. "But if that's all then, well."

"Okay."

I stood and looked around in a panic, thinking of Kevin Burns' triumph when I'd return to the commission. There was a plastic brochure holder on the desk, and I grabbed one of the leaflets, just for something to do with my body.

"End of year summer recital tomorrow night," she said. She was turned back to the computer, but she still watched me as I read the brochure.

"The faculty perform and then the students perform," she added.

"Thanks," I said.

"They are quite amazing."

"No, I'm sure they are. Sorry. One more question. I just remembered it, haha. Who would you tell if you had some sort of disagreement or a conflict with a colleague?"

"I wouldn't know," she said. "I'm not especially disagreeable or conflicting."

I grabbed the office door handle and said, "Yeah. I understand. I'm the same way."

I headed out toward the Metro station on Dupont. Once I was underground, I made some notes in the yellow file and pocketed the performance brochure. By then it was true summer, and I'd taken to Jack Teagarden's version of Misery and the Blues, all about his Share of Sorrows and his claim about how Tomorrow was Always The Same. My only trouble with that song was that it wasn't lyrically accurate, not to me. Because tomorrow wasn't always the same, was it? It was only a tired type of different.

Back in his office later that day I said, "Mr. Burns, I have new information to add to the case. It will warrant the *A* that I've put on there, I think. There were no reporting guidelines. Or procedures at all, really. Employees are not sure of their protections whatsoever. I found nothing, which could really mean something. Right?"

He gave me a vigorous eyeball. And then a nod.

"Another silly girl," he said.

"Sorry?"

"You understand nothing. The absence of evidence against, does not equal existence of evidence for. Just because there is no emergency hotline number does not mean that there never was, or that there never will be. Indeed, the moment you left the place they probably scampered over to the staff room and tacked up some employee rights poster with silly putty and –"

"Yeah, I thought about that, which is why I think we should get back over there as soon as possible."

"There is no WE in PUBLIC SERVICE. Listen to me. You have that information. Go to the show then, indulge yourself. But for now, won't you fuck off? You simply have not stood by the motto of this Commission under my watch, which is *let what will happen anyway, happen already*. And at the beginning I had such faith in you."

So I went.

We have to be careful about where we source our happiness. Have to make sure it's sustainable and all that. And I left with this funny buzz, like a twinkling. Hope? It's hard to tell with that one. It could've just been interest. *Doing* something, you know, instead of waiting around, hoping to have it done to you.

Or maybe I was just really excited to hear the band play.

The idiot inside of me offered India the second ticket.

It was crowded but quiet inside the auditorium. It was dark and atmospheric, the way a real jazz club might be.

Faculty tuned up on stage, and students walked up and down around the aisles with print-out refreshment lists and school merch. Help us support arts efforts in private schools, they mumbled as they waltzed in between sitting adult bodies.

We sat and were approached by a young person. I tried to listen to the tuning going on on the stage. I liked it all, wanted only to be connected to it in some simple way.

"Uh, nothing for me, thanks," I told her. When she didn't move on I realized that fundraising was the done thing around here, and that everybody else around me had plastic cups of wine and beer and coke in their hands, and chips crunching between sips. "Actually," I said. "I'll just take a coke. Thanks."

She handed both India and I a soda can. India's leg jiggled next to mine and I moved my knee away. The acoustics in the auditorium were amazing. I could hear everybody's conversations floating around. I had my yellow case with me, stuffed into a backpack between my legs.

There was a small world in my head that summer which was bent on such deep darkness. But the great ten-piece brass jazz band as it came on stage and started and roared, roared, roared, through the school for a song and then another, that was ecstasy, as though I'd injected it into my bloodstream direct. That was life at sublimation.

On they went, the trumpeter in the front was an angel, and his band was made of angels too, Gabriels, and nothing mattered except that the music should keep on going, and how much I would beg, steal, borrow, kill, to have it everywhere. The way I felt about beautiful music right then was a love that you could see the edges of, like a worried blues note.

I should've known better than to bring India along to that kind of thing.

Her teenage voice, dripping in PA snobbery, flirted through the air where the music fought for space, and landed on my nose.

"Do I have to spend the whole thirty now?" she asked the student in the aisle who'd started to shill out branded sweatshirts and keychains to the row behind us. "Or do you have one of those, maybe, after-pay options?"

India didn't whisper, even though everyone is meant to whisper while the band is on. In fact, I noticed, nobody seemed to really have noticed that the concert had even started. Cash changed hands and teeth crashed into popcorn. Children swapped money for school merchandise, and grown men and women slipped into their new sweatshirts right then and there.

The jazz tried to roar, and I tried to hear it.

"It's actually a cash-only system," the girl said to India.

"Like I want to support the school but who actually uses cash anymore? I have fifteen? What's the point in payin' all now?"

Another young person approached us from a different angle.

"Thirsty?"

"I'm not drinking in a school," India hooted. "I literally go to the school down the road? I think some of my teachers are sitting in this room?"

I stared straight ahead, at the lead trumpet, it should have been beautiful, it was Armstrong: "On the *sunny* side of the *street*."

And all my streets felt sunny, or they might've, could've, should've.

"Do you have any other clothing? Like, other merchandise I mean?"

The student looked on, watched the band play their Armstrong cover too. *"Leave your worries on the doorstep"*— and then she turned back toward India:

"What, like a baseball cap?"

"Yes!" shrieked India, and people started to look around.

Whatever the jazz band had done to me in those first few songs was becoming all ripped up. It blew away, bye bye bye, out of the auditorium and into the city where commuters saw it and chewed it and spit it back out onto the sidewalk. Everybody commuted and chatted and whined my starry music away.

Vera Lynn, Queen of Vocal Jazz, sang ages and ages ago, *"We'll meet again."*

But we wouldn't, me and the music.

"How about a long-sleeve T-shirt?" India pressed. "How much is that?"

"Fifteen," said the student.

"That," said India, and it was the middle of the set now and even the trumpeter drew his eyebrows in, wondered where this entrepreneurial fever had come from. "And two Sprite Zeros, one for my friend. My colleague, actually."

The girl retreated toward the snack booth at the back of the hall, all the jazz and blues gone after her. There was fuss amongst the students attending the merchandise stand as they hunted for items and specific sizes.

I tried to think about all of the angels in music halls. Tried to think about all of the devils that I had meant to catch there, about the phone conversation I'd had the day before, with the woman with the purple eyes.

"I think there might be something to your grievance," I'd told her. "And my boss has consented to allow for further investigation. We could maybe, at least, get through mediation."

"I can't believe how helpful you've been," she had said.

But India whined on. The performers didn't sound like this huge brass band anymore. For a moment they sounded like something out of a punk concert, the type I might have sobbed over when I myself was in high school. And it was The Smiths, talking about Knowing When It's Over. And then quickly back to Blues, even though it had meant to be *jazz*. Right?

So that was when I realized why the Blues is oven hot, frying pan, summertime music, for unlucky summers.

I looked up toward the stage, where the faculty had taken a break to retune. I looked to India, who whore the t-shirt she'd acquired. She looked everywhere except for up at the jazz band.

India asked why I was leaving before the end, but I did not care to answer, because you're not meant to talk while the band is on.

On my way out of the auditorium I thanked the kids who were acting as ushers. When I got outside, I tossed the yellow file marked *A*, with curated notes inside – about the school, about the purple eyed woman, about the absence of a reporting system – into a towering pile of overstuffed trash bags on the street. I watched the papers separate and swirl, and become muddled into those grotesque materials. I thought about the music: How starry it was, how mad it was, how much was mine to ruin.

DREAM COUNTRYSIDE
WEDDINGS

It was a remarkable amount of booze that he put away in ninety minutes, and even more remarkable that it was tequila, and most remarkable of all that his friends and relations hadn't planned for this.

But for now he violently danced. Wedding guests dance with that uniquely weekended way of it, or because everybody else is. His dancing was the opposite: he danced because nobody did. His overhanging stomach, which protruded lovingly through the middle ground between two black suspenders, premeditated the dance moves – first the stomach flung, then the feet followed in the same direction, then the head as an afterthought, but the hand remained steady: it held the drink. There was no music.

Rehearsal dinners like this one incur outrageous expenses and yet so often seem only to serve two types of cheese during appetizer hour (parm and blue) and drinks that are limited to cocktails with titles ("Lovers' Sunrise"). At these kinds of things most everybody is too busy thinking about everyone else to worry about enjoying themselves. Jimmy was not prone to that sort of worry.

This party was bimodal, only two types of people: half afflicted with the disease in the evening time that renders them incapable of dealing with drunks. It's a disease of low tolerance and irritability. And then there were the drunks, who were doing all the irritating. To belong into one or the other is often a product of genetic patronage: at this reception, Jimmy Kernel danced alone as though willed by a higher power, and the surrounding Kernels all laughed at youth having its day (Jimmy was 29), while the Whartons were getting headachy. And it was only 7:15.

Jimmy Kernel's parents were divorced. His father, Teddy Kernel, was a fading alcoholic, but he was still so happy because of how much time he spent on the green, and because he'd never grown out of being an adult called *Teddy,* whereas others might have, by this mid- life point, graduated on to *Theodore.*

Kitty Wharton, Jimmy's mother, weighed eighty-two pounds. The wedding guests enjoyed speculating over her mental illness, or even lunacy. Kitty alone would know and she would talk with nobody about it. At present however, she did not worry about her how her body looked in her formalwear. Jimmy had been dancing like this – dancing, if you asked his father's family, and convulsing, if you asked his mother's – for twenty minutes with little sign of fading stamina, and he now moved toward the microphone that waited atop a carving staircase, for the toasts later on. Kitty watched as he picked up the microphone and burped into it.

"Thank you," he said, and one of the Kernels cousins shouted, "No, thank you!" and Jimmy responded, "Thank *you,* thank you. For this night. I am…you are thankful for this night. The wedding party…where? Where?"

The bridesmaids and best man shrieked from the back of the hall.

"I needed to, ah, to say thanks – and congrats, congrats, to my brother, my big…my big brother. Danny. For the marriage. The *marriage!*"

"They're not married yet!" called the best man. The maid of honor, who held his hand under the table, laughed so hysterically her mascara got all smudged up in the crying.

But Jimmy didn't laugh.

"Who is that? Who the – who the fuck was that? This is a *wedding* – you know, Danny is my brother. Danny is my best man. Who was that?"

As the best man waved up toward Jimmy, who looked in danger of toppling down the stairs, Kitty leaned her knobby chin toward her sister, Hellen Wharton, and said in a mild but vaguely panicked way, "This might turn out like Oxford."

A year prior, the South Carolinian Kernels had landed in the British countryside. They wore wicker flip-flops and suntans and spooky grins. Teddy Kernel led his familial pack out of the chopper, which rested on a concrete slab amidst the blowing grasses and muddy puddles of a field near the hotel. The sun was not a regular around that area of the country. The Kernels leapt onto the fields and splat icy runoff onto their travel wear, tennis whites. They projected an uncomfortable American sunshine across the quiet flatness.

This alarmed and confused the British family of the bride, Mindy, who was to marry Matt Kernel, Jimmy's older brother. The British family tempered this confusion with vodka, because that made sense. It made sense to the Kernels too, in a different kind of way.

It was a lovely ceremony; you would see it in a magazine read by desperate singles. In fact one of the older Kernel uncles, who was in Manhattan publishing, had got the wedding featured in *Twenty Countryside Dream Weddings,* an editorial spread which financially spun out in the Kernels' favor. They'd got a stream of income from the *Countryside Dream Weddings'* readership, born of admiration and jealousy. Something to do with a long time spent reading the article and sifting through their photographs, which generated a lot of ad revenue, which circulated until it landed in their accounts. And this was lucky for them. Because by the time of the feature (in Edition #34), the family's oldest finance pool, sourced from Grandma Kernel's development of Floridian swamplands in the 40's, had slipped imperceptibly away. It might have been slipping for decades before anybody noticed. Years and years later, somebody would ask, quietly, hesitantly, at a wedding ceremony not unlike this one: Where has it all gone? Wasn't there so much of it before? And everybody else would tell him to shut up and just enjoy the party.

The photos in the wedding magazine suggested an ancient love that survived its day and emerged into bright modernity: sparkling Grey Goose centerpieces and a neon photo booth were propped against a mangled tree that stubbornly grew in the center of the "Welcome Field," where champagne flutes awaited guests that pretended to feel unencumbered by how harsh the air felt here – open fields caused wind that bit and mocked. Beautiful beachy women and their beautiful beachy boyfriends, recent graduates that had finished school with the Kernel boys, held champagne glasses but were unable to properly clink them unless under cover of the pavilion tent; cold gusts knocked the glass away. They were made from a sparkling crystalline plastic, lightweight and flimsy, with glitter around the lip that ripped off in patches and attached to sweaty hands, then to thighs wrapped tight in black polyester as guests wiped it off. The wedding photographers were skilled at waiting till such moments passed, and the icy snot no longer dripped onto spray-tans, and guests had a hold of their drinks, and weren't covered in Halloween sparkle. This was when they snapped photographs with editorial potential. The feature in *Twenty Countryside Dream Weddings* was lovely and delicate, screamed of quiet luxury, went viral on social media, where creators hunted for dupes of the glasses and bottles and high heels.

Grandma Kernel had specific instructions for the photographers on the morning of the wedding ceremony:

"If photos of my grandson Jimmy, or the wedding guest named Tom, appear anywhere on your footage, I will personally see you removed from your roles at the publication."

She pointed one short finger, adorned with a white nail as long as the finger itself, toward Jimmy Kernel, who now entered the pavilion in a bowtie, and then toward a skinny man who'd arrived early to secure a far-off seat.

This was Tom, who sat without company. The photographers turned their gaze from Jimmy to Tom and then nodded in unison. Something had gone terribly wrong in the algebraic logarithm that harks over wedding planning – nobody is meant to sit alone like Tom was. The other wedding guests pretended not to notice this void in the seating chart: loners at weddings were injurious and off and made people feel unwanted empathy and guilt that was so tiresome. The Kernels guffawed their way into the tent together. They avoided the seats right around Tom, who was sat near the back of the fluttering tent. So the Kernels were free to sit where they felt that all of this might be a little easier on the nerves: at the front.

Kitty Wharton sensed her ex-husband's arrival before she saw him, a powerful sensory ability that had been inserted into her genome after the divorce. And just after she sensed her husband she sensed his wife, who had – if you asked the Whartons – home wrecked everything. The new wife had started off as Mr. Kernel's secretary before becoming his lover. Kitty spent a long time after that worried that she might become a cliché. This terrified her more than everything else, including her fear of death.

As Jimmy arrived, Kitty nudged her sister Nally, and said: "What is wrong with my son? What is *wrong*?"

If you'd glanced over now toward the Kernel section, at just the right moment, after Teddy patted Jimmy on the back of the shoulder, and Jimmy lifted his head in response, you'd see that no amount of Grandma Kernel's color-correcting foundation could have covered up his determined black eye.

"He shouldn't have come back," Helen said.

"It's his brother's *wedding*," said Kitty.

"Exactly," said Helen. "And how must Tom feel?"

As is often the case with these kinds of weekends, what matters isn't what is happening right now. What really matters is the night before, and what it does to them.

Jimmy was belligerent at the cocktail party on the night before the ceremony. And this—the claustrophobia and hystericism and radio static of the blackout – this was life at full capacity. The uppermost of emotion happened when you felt none of it.

And though Jimmy had much to say, he had trouble with the feeling element, a trouble compounded or solved by booze. He teetered round the party and slogged the rest of his drink, which was vodka on ice with no mix, then danced over to the bar, where the female bartender had seen his approach and shoved a coworker into her place.

"What can I get – " the teenager prompted Jimmy once he'd made it and heaved an elbow onto the bar.

"Seven. Seventy. Seventeen shots," Jimmy looked nowhere. He held up three fingers, and used one finger on the other hand to point at them, then raised his eyebrows at the boy. "Seventeen," urged Jimmy. "I am the greatest…man. I am the best. I am the best man of the wedding."

Six months prior, Jimmy had been told by Grandma Kernel – one of the only ones that would speak earnestly with him in the daytime – that the third brother Danny would be Matt's best man for the British wedding.

"The best man makes it the best wedding for the brother," Jimmy tried. "Seventeen shots for party. For the *wedding* party. And one for my wife."

The female bartender was ducked behind a keg, waiting for Jimmy to lose consciousness. But Jimmy was a tank. He had won the paper plate award for the heaviest weight at his fraternity's final graduation party, where he had blacked out, but not lost consciousness, while some internal intelligence managed to operate the empty vehicle of his body round the party.

"Yes, sir," said the bartender, who started to retrieve glasses. He paused between each movement. There was an older couple waiting to order at Jimmy's right, and they eyed Jimmy not unkindly, in the way recent college graduates look at drunken freshmen, with a kind of reluctant sympathy. Logic told the bartender to serve this couple first.

"What can I get you, sir?" he asked the waiting man.

"One gin and tonic and – what did you want?" Tom looked toward his husband at his side to complete their order, who told the bartender to make that two.

The teenager nodded and grabbed two clean glasses and retrieved Monkey 51 from the top shelf and Fever Tree from the back fridge and scooped ice from the freezer, and in that time Jimmy had dropped his own full glass onto his shoes, watched the shards fly across the pavilion floor, realized this meant he had nothing to drink, roared like the wind outside, grabbed at his hair and shirt buttons in a panic, and look up from all this just as Tom thanked the bartender and handed his husband the second drink.

And Tom was of slight build. His neck fit so effortlessly into Jimmy's reaching claw, as he wailed so loudly it hushed everybody out of their dull conversations, "*This motherfucking little girl and his little girlfriend stole my glass and broke my drink!*"

Jimmy wasn't homophobic – he didn't think enough about other people to be any kind of phobic. Drunk Jimmy, however – he did all kinds of thinking. He thought and thought and thought. So much thinking would capsize anybody. Drunk Jimmy was all types of phobic. And Jimmy seized Tom so suddenly into the air that there was a terrible silence across the party in which everybody felt at once sober and wickedly excited, and they all watched in horror and fascination, until Tom's husband shouted into the silence a mangled plea for a bit of help over here, there's a fight going on. At this, all of the men present remembered their normative duties and started grabbing at shirts and shoving people about, hoping one of them might be one of the two involved, but enjoying the effect either way. Kitty Wharton had been talking to the wedding's officiating Rabbi when Helen hurried over and said, "Kitty, your *son.*"

And just when Kitty looked over, her son had Tom in a

nasty wrestle on the ground, and Mindy British relations had formed a perimeter around the scene, cradling the babies and toddlers away.

It was the groom alone that intercepted the rage at its source. Matt hoisted his brother off Tom, said, "What the *fuck* are doing, Jimmy?"

"He stole my drinks," Jimmy said, and he said it mainly toward his father, who had found his way over, after having missed the breadth of it while lost outside as he tried to find his way back to the entrance. Some time later when this all became a good laugh in retrospect, another guest would ask Teddy where he had been at the moment of the fight, and Teddy in response would ask everybody which celebrity they believed would die before the new year, and whether they'd be willing to bet on it.

"Son." Teddy attempted a lecturing tone that felt factory-created. "You do not respond to this kind of thing with aggression."

"Teddy, he *broke Tom's nose!*" shouted Kitty, who had also materialized.

"Tom stole his drinks," Teddy said in the general direction of his ex-wife.

At the entryway, Grandma Kernel sent the photographers from *Countryside Dream Weddings* home, with instructions to meet with her in the morning before the ceremony, prior to speaking with anybody else.

"It doesn't matter what anybody did!" said Kitty. "Jimmy attacked a wedding guest!"

The bartender watched Tom get led away by peripheral persons that wanted to think themselves helpful. The blood that trickled from Tom's nose and onto his ironed white shirt looked like summer camp tie-dye. Kitty turned toward the Kernel brothers: "How could this have happened? On the night before the *wedding?* What is wrong with you boys? Jimmy!"

But Jimmy had reached his dreamworld. He sat at the perpendicular point where the floor met the bar. It is incredible the limited attention span of certain audiences: Mindy's family had taken their little ones and gone off, but the Kernels had migrated to the other end of the pavilion, where the female bartender worked another bar, and asked who wanted what on what rocks and with diet or regular coke and so on. Already the events of five minutes ago were nostalgic. Remember? Yeah. But barely.

Jimmy, for one, would not – he would not remember in the morning until his grandmother reminded him. His father would never talk about it and Kitty would remember how it felt to be the unfavorable parent and would choose also not to talk about it, in a last-ditch, middle-aged effort to be the cool guardian. And Matt would say to his shaken fiancé on the evening of their wedding: "Don't worry. This never happens," and this would temporarily reassure Mindy about the Americans.

During the ceremony Mindy's parents cried. It might've been because of how beautiful and sweet it all was, or maybe not. Nobody asked.

When they kissed, Tom tried to smile. He thought of his husband in the hotel bed. He'd stayed behind as a form of protest. Tom stopped smiling and looked toward Jimmy, who had found the whole *you may kiss the bride* sequence so uproarious that his cackling shook through the tent and turned the Rabbi's final blessing over the newlyweds' kiss into pure laughter, no religion.

That kind of manic laughter had carried Jimmy all the way through a year, and in that year nothing much had changed apart from another engagement, another wedding season. Everybody that had been present at the British wedding was still alive. Except now, with Jimmy up at the microphone at another cocktail reception, his mother decided to do something about it. She'd been humiliated enough, she thought. By the secretary. By her vacant husband, who'd help to raise these vacant boys.

Kitty grabbed Hellen's arm and said, "I can't let him go on. It'll be like last year in England. Right? I mean, I'm his *mother*."

She stood up and shifted toward her son, who loomed over her on the speech pedestal. She felt Helen's hand pressing her elbow, heard her sister's soft warnings.

"It's not like they don't enjoy it," Helen said. "Seriously. Look."

Kitty looked. She saw everybody looking up at Jimmy, a sort of pre-eminent, baking laughter fermenting around their teeth. Some had already let themselves go into the giggles that they knew would follow. It was an audience that would laugh so hard and for so long you wondered if you might've missed something.

"Just sit down," Helen said. "Why ruin it?"

NEWBORN TRIPLETS

Her belly was bloated, throbbing against her top, and it looked punchable. I wondered whether it had started to kick yet. She wore one of those trendy tops I saw in Pinterest ads. Frilly bows in flimsy knots, not totally tied up, not totally hanging downward. A Hello Kitty charm dangled from her school bag, looked at me with petulance and disdain. It was clear to me that she wanted more than to just be a girl. She wanted to be a baby too.

She was the last to leave when I dismissed the class for lunch, her heavy middle pulling her downward, as if, to her, it carried symbolic weight as well. It all seemed self-indulgent, that slow waddle that she affected, the Hello Kitty charm languishing and sad, like it could feel her dour energy. I knew from the online forums that this was a beautiful thing, that she should be grateful. As *@ttcwfertilityclinicmama* would write, she should feel blessed to be in such a position. Did she know how many women would kill to switch places?

I followed her across the classroom to the door, adapted to her sluggy meander. As she moved, I reached out a hand to feel the pink ribbon tied around her braid. It had frayed edges, hadn't been properly cared for. I'd have cared for it better – lovingly, like I cared for everything.

Uh, Miss? she turned around. Y'alright?

Yes, Hannah, I said. Just making sure the door shuts behind you.

She left the room, and I locked the door behind her and spat in the plastic garbage bin, which had – somehow – already become full of gently-used tampons, all half-soiled with bright blood. The year 10 girls had a weird thing for menstruation that year, wanted to reclaim it, take a sort of ownership of it, and this involved boasting about it to the boys and even sometimes showing them their uterine remains, splashed across sanitary products. They free bled on their jeans, left puddles of little brown clots behind on school chairs. I often noticed that my own was much more clotted than theirs. Theirs was so doused in virginity, reeked in it, which was one reason they were so bent on showing it off.

After Hannah had finally gone, I pulled the rattan basket of newborn clothes out from underneath my desk and laid its contents across a bare table at the back of the room. I searched for imperfections and tears. Here, there were no frayed edges. And although the lace and the gingham and overused cotton were lovely in themselves, it was really the smell of them, sweet and uncurdled. It lingered longer if I didn't put the clothes through the wash, which I'd never do anyway. That would be like killing the girls who'd lived in them before.

At home that night, Braxton looked at me with that particular question on his mouth.

Yeah, I said. I do think I'm ovulating.

But I thought you were ovulating last week, he said.

I think I misread it last week though.

What do you mean, misread it?

What do you mean, what do I mean? I didn't read the app correctly. There's a lot of ways to misread it or even misuse it. Cause it's sensitive, you know. Like there's this woman on the TTC forums, *@ttcwfertilityclinicmama,* who has all of these tricks for properly using the tracker and being as accurate as possible.

Okay. Have you tried any of her tricks?

I try them all the time, Braxton. I'm always peeing on things and holding them at different angles and in different temperatures. It takes time.

Okay. Well, do you feel like you're ovulating?

I don't know. Let me get out up the checklist from the thread. Have I been having mood changes or a change in the position of my cervix?

Uh. I think you should tell me. Like, if I told you, wouldn't that be mansplaining?

I guess. Should we just try anyway?

Afterword, I sank into the duvet and went on a clothing resale app and scrolled in the dark of the bedroom for a long time. I favorited hundreds of baby clothes. I was especially drawn to the Peter Rabbit outfits and anything adorned by the cast of *Winnie the Pooh*. There was a dress-and-bloomers matching set that was labelled 0-3 months and was all in white cotton, its edges laid with white lace, tinged slightly in vintage yellow. Embroidered rabbits peered out of its pockets, and Peter himself, whose father had been long ago baked into a pie, hopped merrily across the chest. One of his ears was flopped over, which I thought was a wonderful detail, lifelike. I messaged the seller.

Would you sell this for $5?

$7 plus shipping.

Ok, I wrote.

The seller didn't respond, so I refreshed the page with the Peter Rabbit bloomers over and over again. Even after several minutes, nobody else had favorited it, which did feel a bit divine.

$6? I wrote.

$6 plus shipping.

Ok, I wrote.

I bought the set and had it sent to the school. Braxton had heard from his mom that it was bad luck to start buying things before you even knew for certain. But I knew that it wasn't about luck, at least not for me. Because for me, there would be no coincidence involved – it was fated.

When it arrived later in the week, I unpacked it in my classroom. I traced its trim, and its lace riddles. Peter Rabbit, there on the front, looked even lovelier now than he had online. I thought of her, wearing the bloomers and the matching dress; she'd be all covered in laughter. And later that night, I thought about the intricate patterns on her newborn clothes, imagined her bundled up and tight-fisted. Most importantly, she needed me desperately, couldn't live without me, all smiles when I popped up from behind a peek-a-boo or concrete corner. Thinking of this, I started to touch Braxton.

Do you think you're still ovulating? he asked.

I don't know, to be honest, I said. I feel like the tracking app isn't accurate. How does it even really know?

It probably does know. Have you asked anyone on TTC? I feel like you should know anyway. It's the same every month. Like, the same feeling. From the checklist?

But I feel a lot of those feelings a lot in the month, I said. I get them confused. Wait. Let me message *@ttcwfertilityclinicmama*. She'll know.

I opened up the thread of messages between her and I. We'd been a part of the TTC forum for a long time, and you get to know certain people who pop up repeatedly in threads, get used to their writing style and private messaging patterns. One good thing about *@ttcwfertilityclinicmama* was that she was always online.

Hey, mama, I wrote. A little conundrum! Lol. Just not sure if our ovulation tracker is working so not sure if it's worth it tonight. What do u think? Any tips on recalibrating tracker? Or maybe should I just get a new one? Ugh!

Her typing dots fluttered on the screen, rising and then falling away again. Finally, she replied.

Hi, mama gal! she wrote. Tbh this is one of those situations where I feel like u should leave it be up to God. He always knows, u know? Like, humans try to discern His will with these devices, but they are no substitute for His truth! Lol! You know what I mean tho?

Totally, I wrote. Thank you mama. Will message you tomorrow same time LOL x

By the time I'd finished on the forum, Braxton was asleep. *@ttcwfertilityclinicmama* was so assured in the way that she looked at life. Lately I had been trying to emulate her. She was always happy because it was always His responsibility. And that felt nice.

In the dark I returned to the same clothing seller's page on the resale app. She had an array of beautiful baby things, clothes and bonnets and nursery furniture. I scrolled through her several hundred posts, and favorited almost all of them. But I avoided any boys' clothes with trite symbolism, like trucks and dinosaurs. All of it so unlovely.

After a while of this, the seller messaged me again.

If you're interested, I can offer you a discount on bundles, she said.

Ok, I said. What is it?

3 pieces for 2 and free shipping.

How many bundles can I do?

As many as u want.

I created several bundles of three pieces each and then rearranged the items around within them so that they were organized by theme. Then, on my own page, I ranked each of my bundles in comparison to the others, to determine which I liked best. It was always the Peter Rabbits. I imagined that she, in wearing so much Peter, might develop a propensity for rabbits, for forest animals generally. Perhaps we could buy her one. A living Peter Rabbit. I think that she would like that.

The next day, Jane and I sat in the communal office, sorting through the mixed mini candies that our boss had brought in. I picked out the pieces that I liked, let some melt on my tongue; stashed a few in my pocket for later. Jane talked through a choking mouthful of sour patch, her pale eyes going red at the rims. She said she'd heard more about the gossip that had been the big news of school lately.

I heard who the father is, she said.

That's a welfare issue, interjected our head of department. If that's true, you need to go to the principal or her head of year.

I don't know if it's true, said Jane. But I think it's probably true.

Who? I asked.

Sebastian. In year 11. Her ex? It makes sense, right? That's what the girls in my year 10 lesson said, that it makes sense, and also that he's, like, abandoning her.

Oh, I said. How far along is she?

Six months or so. My year 10 girls told me that her mom is raging about her deciding to keep it, couldn't believe it, they said. Almost kicked her out of the house. I don't know how she's going to do her exams like this. She won't finish school.

Maybe we can give her some work to do from home, I said. In case she can't come in anymore.

Jane rolled her eyes.

You baby them, she said.

The bell rang and I went to my classroom, settled my year 9s down in their neat rows. An incessant beeping jangled through the still classroom. I called Bena up to my desk, told her to give it up. She placed an ovular electronic device into my open palm.

Miss, she said. It's a Tamogotchi. If you take it it'll die. It's a little pet kind of. I have to feed it and stuff. I have to keep it alive.

I have to hold onto it until one of your parents can come pick it up, I told her.

I didn't like to see those babies so upset, could barely admonish them. Confiscating was painful. I imagined Bena, who was a little teenager already, as she might have been as a small girl; I imagined her in the Peter Rabbit bloomers that I'd bought. She looked lovely in them, but not quite as lovely as mine.

I'm sorry, I continued. When mom or dad comes to school, I'll give it to them.

At the end of the lesson she left the classroom in that terrible state that you see on young people sometimes, where they're trying so hard not to cry.

After she left, I grazed my fingertips over the Tamogotchi's plasticky exterior, all dripping in pink neon. I clicked on the middle of its three buttons, and the screen lit up. A creature crawled, looked out at me. It wasn't any type of animal that I recognized, but it was endearing in the way that it gazed stupidly at me, and so obviously needed human care and reassurance in order to stay alive. I've killed her, I thought. I took away her mother, and so I've killed her.

I packed Tomogachi into my bag and took her home with me that night, brought her under the covers and maintained eye contact, so that she wouldn't feel so alone in her first night away.

Are you interested? Braxton asked when he joined me in the bed.

To be honest, not tonight, I said.

Even after so many years I felt like apologizing after that. I wondered whether this was just conditioning, whether it would stick with me forever. I didn't know at which point this had been bastardized into me, a pathetic need to apologize for sexlessness.

He fell asleep quickly and I picked up Tomogachi from my bedside table, clicked on the screen. She emerged again, and she looked brighter, more hopeful, better-fed, than she had when she'd left her real mother's hands earlier.

Who do you prefer? I asked her. Peter Rabbit or Winnie the Pooh?

She gazed up and bounced a bit. She had two dark circles at the top of her head, not quite ears, but with a similar effect. As she bounced, these bits of flesh bounced with her, floated slightly in short columns on the screen, left behind streams of vanishing pixel.

Okay, I responded. That's fine. There's other stuff like patterns. What about another character? Paddington Bear?

On the resale app, I favorited a onesie embroidered with a Paddington in red rain boots. Then I turned my phone screen toward Tomogachi.

Do you see what I mean? I asked her. There's so many options.

She bobbed up and down more quickly, her fleshy ears waving now in full circles.

Okay, I said. So you like Paddington.

I messaged the seller and asked to put three Paddington items into a bundle, and then that, too, I had sent off to the school.

In class the next day, my year 10 girls whispered about her as they filed in. Nobody likes a whispering teenager. I listened in on their gossip, something that I'm not ashamed of. Teaching is dull work, and hearing about the demented lives of children is one of the few exciting things about it.

I heard her mom is kicking her out, Morgan whispered.

Yeah, said Rachel. She'll have to go into a home or something.

That's so embarrassing, Morgan said, and Rachel nodded her agreement.

They silenced when she walked in, in the type of way that's meant to be obvious. Her belly was even bigger than it had been the previous week. That seemed impossible, even alarming. Was she going to her doctor's appointments? Was she able to have her ultrasounds, take her prenatal vitamins? There seemed something very off about her belly, its largeness, its gargantuan self-evidence.

After class, I called her up to my desk.

Is everything going okay? I asked.

She rolled her eyes.

No offense, Miss, she said. But all the teachers are asking me that now. And it's not as if anybody asked me that before.

Okay, I said. Well, I have a lot of prenatal gummies. I keep them in my desk so that I remember to take them in the morning. Here's an unopened pack. They're shaped like owls. And the flavors are nice. Take them.

Thanks, she said. Miss, are you...?

No, I said. But probably really soon.

Hannah left with the owls, and later that afternoon once school was over, Bena's mom showed up for her daughter's Tamogachi. Of course, this exchange demanded total professionalism and reserve, as if sweet Tamogachi had only been a set of air pods. When Bena's mom put the little one into her bag and left the classroom, I messaged *@ttcwfertilityclinicmama*.

Ugh, I wrote. Sometimes I feel like I'm so close and then it just goes away, u know.

That's so normal, mama gal, she responded. Honestly, it will all happen in His time!! No use trying to work around it tbh ☺

I think that's so true, I responded, and then I logged off to go home.

The following day, Bena came up to my desk a bit enraptured.

Thank you, Miss, she said. For keeping her alive.

That's okay, I said. That's what I'm meant to do.

And I believed this so ardently that I'd ordered three brand-new Tamogachies online, which arrived quickly. These new daughters took some of the misery out of the loss of my original. I missed her, but I'd felt a bit of a fraud in my caretaking – I got the perpetual sense that, although she liked and appreciated me, she missed her real mother. And who could blame her for that?

Because I had three little ones now, they needed names.

I scrolled through my Notes App where I kept an ongoing list of baby girl names for the future and selected my favorites. Then I decorated each little rotund device in a different-colored ribbon. Nobody likes to be coalesced with their sisters, and they each deserved their own identities, to be their own individual little girls.

That night, I was so busy with the three new Tamogachies that I didn't do any resale app scrolling. Three was a lot of work, but I'd always known that that would be true. It didn't frighten me – I answered the call, I think, with grace. That's the type of word that I see thrown around a lot on the TTC forum, and also *@ttcwfertilityclinicmama* frequently advises me to handle all things with grace, which seems like a reasonable goal.

The next morning, the girls and I were all fatigued. One had had colic and another, fits of wailing. The third slept peacefully till her sisters woke up screaming. I tried to coax and nurse them in their morning misery, because I, like so many mothers on the forums, put them before me – even when I was ravaged by fatigue too. As I cooed to them, Braxton woke up and started to touch me. While he did this, I soothed one of the sweet Tamogachies, the one in a gingham ribbon that reminded me of summers from a long time ago. I checked on her food levels and did the same for her sisters. He continued to touch around my panties, which felt invasive, maybe even a bit predatory, to do in front of little girls.

Uh, I said. I'm really not in the mood.

He turned around and I felt no impulse to apologize.

Before school that day, my phone lit up with a message from *@ttcwfertilityclinicmama.*

Mama, she wrote. I cannot believe this but I think I tested pozzie. Literally what?! I'm so over the moon and ecstatic I could cry. It was all in His time!!

OMG, I wrote. That is crazy. Because same! I feel it too, inside me. I literally feel like a mother all of a sudden, in a new way. What a coincidence! I could cry.

She sent back a stream of wailing emojies and pink hearts.

Tamogachies came to school with me that day. I'd done enough reading on the forums to know that little ones – especially newborns – need to be tended to and fed at constant intervals. One could not really trust a male partner in these sorts of things. They sat sweetly on my desk in a row of three, their screens blinking up and fleshy ears bouncing. I brought out the clothing basket so full of gently used wares. The Tamogachies drowned in them, of course. But they'd soon grow into them. Before I could even blink! I attempted to appreciate the moment as I was in it. I thought they looked lovely and pristine, their small oval screens perched at the neck holes of three white dresses. One shivered a bit, sniffed her nose.

Here, I said. Let me put this on you, sweet girl.

It was a soft jumper, Peter Rabbit embroidered around its collar, which fit so daintily around her little screen head.

Do you like him? I asked her. Peter Rabbit?

She bounced in her sweet way.

My year 10 girls came in then, resumed their whispering, and silenced when Hannah emerged in the doorway, her elephantine belly distended from her body awkwardly, like a parasite. Today, the girls could only stare.

Hannah, I called after everybody had filed out. Come here for a moment.

When she was at my desk I asked if there was anything else that I could do for her. I'm pretty well-versed in maternal matters, to be honest, I said. And pre and postpartum, things like that. Look. I have this amazing collection.

And I pulled out the rattan basket, stuffed full of baby clothes in different shades of white. That smell of dusty milk and soft skin reached her quickly, I could see it, could see it drift in and occupy. Then there was a new sparkle in her, something devious, like she wanted to steal. She reached out a greedy paw and stroked the blue embroidery of a Peter Rabbit bloomer set.

Wow, Miss, she said. Can I have this?

What?

What? I thought that's what you were doing.

Her hand retreated, folded itself into the front pocket of her babyish sweatshirt, stained in iced coffee and sugar.

Hannah, I said. I have my own to look after.

She only shrugged, said, I didn't realize. Slugged her way out of the classroom like she always did, with the parasite on her belly hanging and mocking.

In the department office I explained to Jane what had happened.

She asked for hand-outs, I said. As if we have anything to spare, right.

They can be so entitled, Jane agreed.

Hannah didn't come to class for several days after that.

I think she's had it, Morgan whispered to the listening girls. I wonder if she's giving it away.

I wondered too. Did I have room, space in my heart? In

my bed? My own girls were growing quickly, teething, sapping me dry. Their wails through the night sounded very painful, and my cooing didn't work as well as it had during the newborn phase. The forums suggested that this was normal, a sleep regression that all babies go through. They encouraged me to keep going, mama.

So I did. The triplets came with me everywhere, slept in my desk drawer while I taught rote lessons. Jane appeared in my doorway one afternoon.

She's had it, she announced. My year 10s told me.

How beautiful, I sympathized.

Grading kept me at school late that night, so I assumed my working mama hat and tried my best to be everything at once.

I received a message from *@ttcwfertilityclinicmama*.

False positive, she wrote. To be honest, it's shaking my faith. Nothing has ever made me question my faith like this before. Cause when is it my time, you know?

So sorry mama, I sympathized. Horrible to hear. But yes, all in His time though. I might not be able to write so often tho, mama. I'll be v busy. Just found out it's multiples!!!

She didn't respond after that.

By nighttime the school was empty, so I took them out and clicked them on. I perched them back into their outfits, their plasticky exteriors shaped like perfect, ovular heads.

I felt my breasts fill and weep. I brought the first baby to me and it began to suck.

LESSONS IN DISSECTION

Over the weekend, another brick was thrown through Dr. Amis' office window. Lately the principal had kept his personal confines heavily guarded. He'd brought in a security man, whom he called a Student Resource Officer. I suspected that this figure was, more than anything, a member of the local police, and I did suspect that he carried a gun. This policeman patrolled the halls around Dr. Amis' office with a clubfooted determination. He looked like he'd once been a high school hall monitor. Very into his own power in that particular way that you tend to see looming so large in certain school buildings.

"So," Jane said. "They obviously figured out when the Student Resource Officer wouldn't be around. And they threw it from the outside, right. Cause Dr. Amis' cop only guards his office from the *inside*."

"I thought the school grounds are locked up at the weekend," I said. "Nobody can really get in without being noticed eventually, I think. They'll find him soon."

"No," Jane said. "And Him? I'd be willing to bet you that it's the year 10 girls."

"It does tend to be them," I agreed. "But brick-throwing feels, you know, aggressively boyish."

"Like, girls choose lighter weapons?"

"Yeah, or maybe no weapons at all. Some other tactic. And they do better planning, maybe."

"I feel like it was well-planned, to be honest."

"We'll find out soon, I guess."

Jane left our department's office room. I watched her slide into the doldrums of the school hallway, which stank of rotting food and fruity perfume infused with glittery particles. The glitter sat on the girls' throats and collarbones, emphasizing their loveliness, exacerbating my asthma. They all bought their perfume from lingerie stores at the mall, the ones smothered in pink and polka dot motifs, stores that constantly claim bankruptcy and then re-emerge. The body sprays come in boxy plastic bottles, and when the girls spray a very particular amount of it across their bodies, it puts an umami feeling in the root of my teeth. I suddenly need to eat a steak. That feeling in my teeth surged as I followed Jane out the office door, let myself get caught up in the body spray snare.

"We're starting our dissection lessons today," I announced at the start of my afternoon class. A few of the students with weaker constitutions made disturbed noises. Most of these were girls. The boys were excited about the world of dissection. A boy named Jack flexed his hand in the front row.

"Form small groups and choose a lab table," I said. They folded into their partitions like they always did, the boys shoving one another to get a look at the specimens, and the girls acting pointedly aloof, to suggest that there was nothing much here to care about.

There was a group of year 10 girls in that lesson who consumed so much lingerie shop body spray that they often suffocated within it. They insisted upon drenching themselves so completely, and so they choked on it when it overtook the air in small rooms, and it made their arms and necks look so wet. They gathered around a lab table at the back of the room and brought with them a wave of artificial fruit smells. Upon the table a gray piglet lay on its side.

Across the six lab tables, the dead piglets were identical. You could choose very precise coloring and chemical dispositions and biological functions and sizes and ages when you checked out online, and I liked to keep the little babies all the same, as a sort of solidarity thing. For instance, I always chose girls, because if I were a girl pig, I'd want to be surrounded by my girlish peers. The pigs also all shared the same strange smile, because of how their snouts upturned and their lips dug deep into their prepubescent faces. Their thick tongues jutted out in a determined way that I've not seen in living pigs. But the best part was their eyes, which were always closed, frozen in what looked like the last moment of a soft eyelash flutter.

The girls crowded around their pig, swapped chap sticks in pastel tubes.

"I'm literally not touching that thing," Joanne said. There was a general agreement. "I feel like this should be illegal," she added.

"We could, like, protest it," Ashley suggested. "Cause isn't it like inhumane?"

"Miss," Katy called from their conglomerate. "Is this, you know. Humane?"

"Of course, girls," I said. "They only use unborn piglets whose mothers are dead. And the piglets are dying or dead too, when they take them. They'll have health issues if they let the pigs live. So, they collect them from free-range farms when it's time for them to die. This way they can contribute to science in death. It's actually an honorable end for a piglet."

This was in some ways true and in some ways not. The fetal pigs were delivered yearly, preserved in formaldehyde.

When they arrived, they looked suspended in that clear poison, usually upended in the dead middle of the specimen bag that contained them – and until they were freed from their plastic formaldehyde homes, they looked to be floating in a perfectly clear womb, their hooves splayed out before and behind them, in mid-flight run.

This the students knew. They saw me unpack the piglets from their deliverances, watched as I demonstrated the correct disposal process for formaldehyde, a teachable moment, I thought, about chemical substance safety. It was a more delicate matter, of course, that the piglets didn't come from some bucolic Eden but instead from the local sausage production plant, ripped from bellies in a just-before-birth state, when it was time for their mothers to be ground up and encased. This isn't the sort of thing that you tell a fifteen-year-old-girl. Instead, I liked to construe Wilber-esque visions for their pliable imaginations, sweet pastoral worlds in which anthropomorphic animals got along and stood against evil together.

"Start filling out your tool kit list," I said. "And write out your plans for our three dissection lessons. You'll need to identify all of her biological systems."

"It's a girl," a boy whispered to his group. There was twittery excitement then. "Miss, since it's a girl, can we –"

"No," I said. "Writing now."

They didn't do any real dissecting that lesson, only got used to the look of the piglets and learnt the names of their silver tools. That smell that always accompanies the fresh bodies started to ache in the air above the lab tables. The year 10 girls in the far corner pulled out their body spray and unleashed it on themselves, their friends, and the piglets.

"That's better," Joanne commented.

They filed out at the bell, and I started the work of hiding the piglets away before my next class. Some groups had already started to mark them up, used imprecise sharpie lines to outline anatomy and note incision locations. In the process a few of the piglets had got a bit twisted, a hoofed little leg bent behind a back, or a pointy snout ripped slightly too far open at the end of a precariously angular neck – students were sometimes surprised to see that the piglets had teeth, which is an option that you can choose when you check-out from the wholesale website, a selection from a series of possible fetal development stages. Jane had been the one to walk me through this process when I'd agreed to take on biology lessons.

"You always want to select the *pail* option at the end," she'd advised. "Cause then they give you a pail of ten, it's like buying in bulk. So it's cheaper that way."

I covered the piglets in preservation paper, slipped them into drawers underneath the lab tables. At the girls' table, I used a paper towel to wipe away spots of sticky glitter from the piglet's protruding belly. Then I licked my finger and ran it around a fleshy hoof that had also caught the residue of pink body spray. Once it looked in better condition I tucked it into its drawer, opened the windows of the classroom to dissipate that smell of iron and babies.

The next week Jane came into the office looking like there was gossip. "It happened again," she said. "But listen. I don't know how to tell you this. It might be bad."

"What?" I said. "Tell me."

"Another brick went through Dr. Amis' window this weekend," she said. "Shattered it, landed on his carpet."

"Okay," I said. "Isn't this like the third time this month?"

"Sort of," she said. "But this one had a pig attached to it."

"A pig?"

"No, not a real one. Like, a fetal piglet."

"What, like the ones we get from Lopez's Preserved Fetal Pigs?"

"Obviously. Where else can they get them?"

"Online, probably? Amazon?"

"I'm just saying," she said. "Dr Amis is furious. I actually heard him telling his Student Resource Officer to patrol the science hallway, and he was yelling that when he catches the student, he'll preserve them. In formaldehyde. Like the pig."

There was a panic then, and I left Jane behind, ran to my classroom, where I was glad to find the door locked as it had been when I'd left on Friday evening. I went through the drawers under the lab tables, checked that each pig was present, the exact same fetal piglets that the students had left behind. I waited then, trying to fend off a feeling in my stomach that arose every time I was near Dr. Amis.

He appeared at the glass doorway as I knew he would, the only person in the school who wore a suit and tie every day. The pants fit poorly, were too long for his small stature, and they hanged over his shoes. But they accentuated his thighs, all swollen like puffed-up meat. He spoke like a historian on a Tudor family documentary, nasal undertones and self-importance, like he went to a lot of dinner parties in rooms with well-thought-out ambiance.

"A moment of your time," he said, as he came in and paced up to my desk, laid both hands flat on the surface. "There's been a breach."

"I think I've heard, sir. I've already checked. All of my piglets are accounted for, and my room was locked this morning. I always lock it when I leave. Nobody could have come in."

"Where does a child get a well-preserved fetal piglet?"

"Well," I said. "Maybe anywhere, really. I think they can get anything online these days."

The Student Resource Officer stood just outside the closed classroom door, his back to us.

"There is something going on here," he said. "Something going on. I can feel it. I have a sense for these things. Discontent and general stupidity amongst the student body. In the air. Some kind of insolence, or rebellion. I knew it was coming again."

He walked around to the lab tables, ripped open one of the piglet drawers.

"This is the same piglet," he said. "The same piglet that came through my window. And it shattered the glass. Because it was attached to a brick. It shattered the glass window of my office. Again. And I suppose I'll tell you what you may already know. Preserved fetal piglets carry a certain stench."

"It can't be the same, Dr. Amis. These were locked in here all weekend."

"Jesus Christ. Not the same *piglet*. The same type of piglet."

"Oh," I said.

He slammed the drawer shut. I felt that I could hear the piglet's hooves clatter around a bit inside.

"What are you teaching them?"

"Just how to dissect the pigs, sir. For the anatomy unit."

"And what else?"

"I'm sorry?"

"I said what else."

He was blustering now, his words bouncing loudly across the lab space. The Student Resource Officer turned his shoulders toward us very slightly.

"Just anatomy. It's for the biology curriculum."

"Something isn't right in this classroom. And something isn't right with you. I can always tell. I can see it in teachers' eyes, when there's something not quite right. There is something failing inside of you."

His voice rose throughout the course of this monologue, so that by the end he sounded like he was singing. He thrust across the classroom in the way he always does, eyes and chin and neck first, to smell out wrongdoing. And he slammed the door behind him so that even the dead piglets in their drawers rattled and felt it.

Dr. Amis' shattered window was replaced that same day, like it had been every time before this. Rumors danced around the hallways. One narrative prevailed about something haunting Dr. Amis, something that wanted revenge. The students were in a flurry when they came in for their dissection lesson.

"Miss," Joanne claimed. "One of the piglets from the lesson broke into Dr. Amis' office. That's literally crazy."

"Why do you think she did it?" Ashley asked.

"Maybe they're not totally dead when they arrive, I think."

At this some of the other groups started to stick pencils down their own piglets throats, pushing past their little teeth, as if to awaken them from their near-death.

"This has nothing to do with you all," I announced. "Nothing. Our pigs are all accounted for, and somebody is playing a sick joke. Actually, it's vandalism. Stop thinking about it. We're starting to dissect today."

The prospect of the first day's dissection seemed to quell their musings about a ghost fetal pig. But things got worse after that. Three weeks passed and my students had finished with their dissections. The smell had gotten worse as the pigs were taken apart, as groups removed organs or intestines for identification. You weren't really meant to know that it had ever been a pig at all, by the end.

But over those weeks, three fetal piglets crashed into Dr. Amis' office window, attached to bricks. Always over weekends, and the window was always fixed by the end of the day on Monday. There were no more pigs in my room, not even their carcasses or innards. Even the smell had almost gone. Nobody could have taken my fetal pigs. Nobody at all.

This wasn't evidence enough for Dr. Amis. On the third Friday after the third window-shattering, he came again to my classroom door.

"A moment of your time," he said.

"Yes," I said, but he was already before me, standing above my low desk chair.

"There is something deeply amiss about you. Something with these pigs. You're not a teacher. What you really are is a failure. Something very demented going on in here. Whatever you're doing in here is an embarrassment to the institution of education."

"Sir —?"

"Now she talks!"

"I don't know what's going on with the piglets or the bricks, sir. I don't know. I don't even have any pigs left. We used them all up for anatomy."

"You're just becoming a failure. Like a lot of teachers here. What sort of teacher works in such revolting ways? You're brutal. Like I said. Demented. And failing, truly. Failing the kids. Failing *me*. What is it, to be such a failure? Do tell. What is it like?"

But have you ever been called a failure like that? With a sense of pure objectivity, like he's completely got to the truth of it? And have you ever heard it from a small man with a terrible voice? I didn't think there was much else to say. A lot of me agreed with him, and so I relented, so full of agreement and respect and admiration for this small man and his largess ideas. Because perhaps he really had got the right of me.

"I am," I said. "I am I am I am."

"Yes. A failure indeed."

He stalked out of the room then, and linked up with his policeman. School was over for the weekend, and the hallways had hushed. There was nobody else around, so I thought about what other people might do in this situation. I tried to make myself cry, succeeded after a while, but it didn't feel quite right.

That weekend the student who'd been flinging the bricks and the pigs finally sang their swan song and set fire to the principal's office. School was cancelled on the Monday, even though the arson had been only small, the true work of a juvenile. It had turned to rubble the windows lining Dr. Amis' office, warped his desk and computer into blackish tendrils. This all I heard from Jane, to whom I'd given my resignation letter, asking her to turn it into Dr. Amis as a favor.

Unemployment has been nice if a bit grey. There's a few weeks until summer, and when all of that ends so too will the teaching contract. Now I'm on something described as *health leave,* which was granted after I called the hospital and pretended to be a woman in the throes of a mental breakdown. So during night times I haunt the village, sometimes crying in weird tones. There's nowhere to go in the morning, so I can do that now. I walk miles and miles from our village to the ones just over there, on the badly lit suburban sidewalks. Nothing happens and nobody notices. There are so many schools around, many of them beautiful. A colonial mansion for elementary school students, with wide white columns that students of that age can't really appreciate for their loveliness. There are recently remodeled high schools, all transparent walls and ceilings, open spaces and slim computers. Their welcome signs describe them as campuses, not just any school building. They have all sorts of different parking lots. There's private schools on the edges of towns, brick and ivy, with bell towers and quadrangles and weeping willows. You don't have to go there in the daylight to know that all of the students are beautiful and symmetrical.

Sometimes I go around to my old school, of course. From most angles the school looks just the same as before. But there's a way to slip into school grounds, by following a dark trail that lines the high fence around the building's perimeter. Follow it for long enough and you'll come to a nearly imperceptible ditch in the dirt underneath the fence, where teenage bodies have sprawled and clawed and dug for so long that it's become a dirty little tunnel. This takes you right below the fence and spits you out at the building's front corner, where the tomb of Dr. Amis' old office is now. They put up a tarp to hide the damage, perhaps to drive off copycats. Students use this route to go in and around their school in the nighttime, something that they must find thrilling and provocative.

I know what you're thinking. *I know*. Things aren't looking good for me. Not with the other things. Everything might point to my culpability. But sometimes things just work out, no intervention needed. And do you know what? They have a lead, Jane's told me. They found that one of my Year 10 girls was a little too fascinated by the fetal piglets, how they were obtained and killed and what sorts of conditions their mothers lived in before death. She really botched their interrogations, admitted to all sorts of gruesome search engine tunnels about the life and death of a fetal she-pig. It must be her. It does make some sense. And when it's proven she'll be expelled, might actually go to court. Dr. Amis' Student Resource Officer could arrest her, right in the heart of the school building.

I'd been wrong, thinking that it must have been a boy. Totally underestimated the fury in the heart of a girl, the single-minded destructive impulse that can permeate and deprecate. So what am I to do if she's done for arson? Become a fangirl? I could write her a letter in juvenile detention, an anonymous admirer. Echo the sentiment that she's not so alone, not really. Thank her for helping everything along. Because thanks to that unhinged and maniacal girl, things are really starting to look up for me.

And now at night I can go back to the school grounds through the gate and sit on the dewey grass and smile at the black, hollowed out office. It is now being rebuilt in a safer space, somewhere deep in the womb of the school.

THE AUTHOR

Heather Colley is an English Literature PhD student at Oxford University and a research fellow of the British Library. Her fiction writing has won *The Oxford Review of Books* Short Fiction Prize, the Hopwood Award, and the Desperate Literature Short Fiction Prize Shortlist. Her academic work has won the D.C. Watt Prize and been published in *Review of English Studies, Routledge Companion to Gender and Childhood,* and *Oxford Comparative Criticism and Translation Review*. Her debut novel *The Gilded Butterfly Effect* was published by Three Rooms Press in October 2025.